The Baby Machine

ANN MAJOR

D1079083

SILHOUETTE®

*Silhouette and Colophon are registered trademarks of
Harlequin Books S.A., used under licence.*

*First published in Great Britain 1995
Silhouette Books, Eton House, 18-24 Paradise Road,
Richmond, Surrey TW9 1SR*

© Ann Major 1994

ISBN 0 373 04929 3

54-0802

*Printed and bound in Spain
by Litografia Rosés S.A., Barcelona*

A Note from Ann Major

Because I was deeply in love with my husband when he asked me to marry him, I said yes in the next breath. Then he said he wanted five children, and I said, 'I don't want any.' Not that I didn't like babies. I just felt too young and immature to assume such responsibility.

After we'd been married a year, Ted pressured me to get on with producing the longed-for brood. To convince me that having a baby was easy, he insisted that I watch one of his patients in the delivery room. Since the woman had already had eight children, he figured the delivery would be a snap.

What men don't know about women could fill volumes of romance novels. The poor woman couldn't have screamed louder if you'd thrown her naked to a starving group of grizzly bears. Needless to say, another year passed before I would even allow him to whisper the word *pregnancy*.

When I finally did give birth to our first son, I felt as proud as a queen who'd produced a long-awaited, royal heir. I instantly felt committed to Ted in a new and profound way.

Romance for me has never had much to do with candle-lit dinners and champagne, but everything to do with the connection of two people on emotional, spiritual and physical planes. So, for me, watching a football game with my husband can be a very romantic kind of thing. Just driving to the school to pick up one of our kids—together—seems sexy and romantic. Thus, I don't feel our children have interfered with our romance as much as they have enhanced it because of the deeper emotional texture they have brought to our relationship.

Of course, as a young mother I always insisted that my children take naps every afternoon from two until five. Not that they always slept, mind you, but the little dears did dutifully stay in their rooms and were silent—even Kimberly, even when she was a terrible two.

Everyone thought I selfishly wanted that time to write, and I did…weekday afternoons. But on the weekends when Ted was home… Guess again.

Ann Major

To Tara Gavin
Again! And Again! And Again!
All my books should be dedicated to her.

Chapter One

Anger and grief burned through Jim Keith Jones like acid as he set the chain saw down and picked up the ax. In six days, that rich vulture, Kate Karlington, would repossess what to her was probably just another motley collection of real estate, but what to him was a lifetime of dreams and hard work.

He'd built his little empire from scratch—vacant lot by lot, house by house, building by building. He'd painted and hammered and mowed and hauled trash—there hadn't been a job he'd been too good to do to keep his properties up for his tenants.

Next Friday, Karlington would smilingly pick his bones clean and leave him for dead. Only, he wouldn't be dead; he'd be groveling in the gutter where he'd started, alive with the bitter reality that he had failed again.

Karlington wasn't the only reason his mood was so foul. It was May, a month that could be oppressive in Houston because so many days were as white and humid and smotheringly hot as this one. But today was especially dreadful because three years ago to the day he'd buried Mary on a muggy afternoon like this.

Jim Keith's filthy sleeveless sweatshirt was drenched with perspiration. His curly black hair was glued to his tanned brow. His dark eyes were bloodshot from the ravages of the binge he'd gone on the night before. His damp ragged jeans clung so tightly to his hard thighs, the navy denim looked as if it was painted on.

Slowly, carefully, his powerful brown arms lifted the ax and then sank it into the rotten trunk with all the savage vengeance his lean muscular body was capable of. When the blade crunched into soft wood, his perfectly sculpted mouth grimaced as if razor-edged steel had sliced through his skull. No wonder. He had a six-star hangover. He had celebrated the anniversary of Mary's funeral by tying one on.

He had gone home last night and drunk his dinner and watched home videos of Mary until he'd passed out. He did that every time her birthday and their wedding anniversary rolled around, too.

This morning he'd awakened to a fuzzy white television screen, crawled to his refrigerator, drunk a single beer, brewed a pot of black coffee and scrambled a mountain of eggs. Then he'd showered and driven to his sister Maggie's house and dutifully picked up his nine-year-old son, Bobby Lee, who had tearfully begged him to let him sleep in or watch cartoons instead of taking him to some apartment complex to work. Not that Bobby Lee ever did much.

Father and son were now hard at work cleaning up Jim Keith's worst apartment project, which was located just off the Eastex Freeway in a crime-ridden neighborhood populated with low-income families. Or rather, Jim Keith was working. Bobby Lee never really did much.

But even after a morning of mowing and chopping

and weed pulling, Jim Keith still felt like death warmed over.

On her deathbed, Mary had begged him to be strong.

Dear God he'd tried.

He swung the ax again, and wood chips flew as the blade bit into the trunk. For three long years he'd tried. But every night when he finished work, the demons of loneliness and dark grief still haunted him. It was all he could do to get through the days and nights, all he could do to go through the motions of being a father, of being a businessman.

Of being a human.

But he was losing it.

In those last months before her death, he hadn't cared about anything except saving Mary. He hadn't thought of his future or his son's, and because he hadn't, he'd borrowed money and taken Mary to Germany in the hopes of finding a miracle cure that his insurance wouldn't pay for. That was why he was badly overextended. That was why, despite his economizing over the past three years, despite his working seven days a week, come Friday he was really going to lose everything, even the roof over his head, to Karlington.

While oil revenues, property values, and job opportunities had plummeted, utility bills and property taxes had soared. Thus, the Houston real estate situation had deteriorated dramatically. Entire office buildings were fenced off and vacant. Thousands of apartment buildings had been bulldozed and the land sold for next to nothing. Entire neighborhoods of foreclosed houses sat empty. Banks had failed. Things were turning around now, but it was too late for him.

The economic situation would have been precarious for any man, but it had proved too much for a heavily indebted man devastated by the death of his beautiful young wife. Karlington had swooped down like a scavenger and bought his notes at a humiliatingly low, deeply discounted price. Nothing could save him from her—nothing short of a miracle.

And he'd lost faith in miracles when Mary died.

He wouldn't have bothered to clean up the project today, since it was as good as Karlington's, except wielding the ax was therapy.

The blade sliced one final time into the soggy trunk, and the rotten pecan tree groaned, toppling with a violent thud to the spongy, overgrown lawn.

He pitched the ax into the weed-choked flower bed beside his wheelbarrow and scanned the empty grounds for Bobby Lee. Jim Keith frowned when he saw the abandoned trash can and the door to number 20 sagging open. He'd ordered Bobby Lee to pick up everything inside and out of that apartment two hours ago. It was a thirty-minute job at best even for Bobby Lee, who moved as slow as molasses, but it looked as if Bobby Lee hadn't even spent five doing it.

Since Bobby Lee liked cars, Jim Keith headed toward the parking lot. Jim Keith's frown deepened as he considered Bobby Lee's laziness. The kid took after the Whits, Mary's easygoing bunch, most of whom were lazy as hell and hadn't amounted to much. Not that they cared. They got through life on charm. Maybe he shouldn't worry. When they found life too tough, most of them married well.

Mary herself had been no fireball. But she'd more than made up for it by being so pretty and sweet and fun-loving—and so damned good in the sack. She'd loved him since they'd been kids. His friends had teased him about the way she'd chased after him down the halls in high school.

"Oh, hi there, Jimmy," she'd purred from behind him, acting as if she was surprised to see him even though she was breathless from her breakneck run. When he'd turned around, she'd tossed her nose in the air so that her gold straight hair danced on her shoulders. Then she'd casually smiled up at him as if she wasn't especially anxious to see him after all. So then, of course, he'd had to prove himself and chase her. She'd known how to set the hook, let him nibble just a bite or two to get a delicious taste, before she snapped the line good and tight.

They'd been petting one night, and he'd wanted her so badly he couldn't wait. And she'd said, "Jimmy, you can't have me unless you marry me."

"Is that a proposal, baby?"

She'd giggled. "Now that you mention it—"

He'd started the car and driven hell-bent for Mexico. The old car had died at the border. They'd had to walk across the bridge and look for an official to marry them. Neither of them was even eighteen. They'd sold the car for scrap and hitchhiked back to Houston. He'd paid the first month's rent with the money from the car and dropped out of high school and started working harder than he'd ever worked.

Mary had always praised everything he'd done. Somehow he hadn't cared that she was so disorganized and never got much done. He'd loved her. God, how he'd loved her. They'd had tough times, but they'd made it. Until she'd gotten sick. Until he'd failed to save her.

Never again would he let himself fall in love. Because bright as the years with her had been even when they'd been poor as dirt, her illness and death had taught him about the dark and terrible price of love.

He scowled when he reached the parking lot and saw it was empty. Now where the hell was Bobby Lee?

Jim Keith was about to turn around when he saw the gleaming perfection of a dark green Jaguar gliding smoothly beneath the towering pine trees.

Then he stopped dead in his tracks when he recognized the woman behind the wheel—Kate Karlington.

Not that she'd recognize a lowlife like him. But he knew what she looked like, from seeing the society columns in the newspaper.

Fighting the murderous rage building inside him, he shrank behind the wall of his building as she stealthily parked her car under a towering cottonwood. High on her own success—her inherited success—she thought she knew everything and was always writing columns in the Houston papers about how to succeed in a recession. If she was so smart, how come she drove a car like that to this neighborhood and risked it being stolen or stripped?

She had her nerve, too. He'd had her served with

a peace bond to stop her from snooping around his projects and harassing his managers. If he called the cops now, they'd haul her to jail. The thought of the elegant know-it-all Kate Karlington handcuffed and on her way to the clinker brought out the wicked white grin that had captured Mary's heart.

When the regal-looking young woman coolly unfolded her long, slim body from the car, holding a briefcase, his wolfish grin deepened. Then his eyes skimmed over her angrily—top to bottom.

Why did she have to be so damned beautiful?

His heart began to pound like a sledgehammer, and no longer solely from anger. The hot day seemed to press in on him harder than ever. It wasn't even noon, but he felt an odd, unwanted hunger.

Which only made him hate her all the more.

Black-and-white pictures didn't do her justice.

Mary had been soft and gentle and golden. This witch's beauty was so strong and bold and opulently charismatic, it struck him like a body blow even at this great distance. Her hair was shiny coils of vivid flame caught in a green silk scarf at her nape. She had the kind of figure a man who didn't despise her would die to get his hands on—lush breasts, a narrow waist, curving hips and long legs. She had a brisk walk that told him she was a woman of immense energy.

In the bedroom he imagined she would be volcanic.

Why the hell had his mind wandered to the bedroom?

Kate wore a green silk blouse and green linen slacks. He noticed the crisp, starched look of those slacks. They had obviously been ironed within seconds of being put on. Precisely applied and dramatic makeup darkened her eyes and made her lips brighter.

He found he couldn't take his eyes off her till she disappeared around the back of his building. But that was only because the sneaky bitch was his enemy.

No way was he calling the cops.

No way would he forgo the pleasure of teasing and torturing her himself.

Chapter Two

Kate Karlington, who was reputed to have inherited her father's cold but very shrewd business mind, was fastidious to a fault. Above all she appeared *in control*. Her curly red hair was tightly pulled back; her linen slacks crisply pressed. Every business document in her briefcase was tidily filed by subject and date. Every square in her calendar was carefully marked with her plans for that day.

Her teachers and her strict father had severely punished her for inefficiency, sloppiness and neglect, and she had learned their lessons well. Thus, when she stumbled in one of Jones's potholes in his poorly paved parking lot and got a run in one of her expensive stockings, she frowned impatiently. She paused to study the ruinous neglect of Jones's forlorn-looking buildings. Pink bricks were blackened from mildew. Several broken windows were taped.

Neglect ate into profits. She deplored greedy, shortsighted landlords like Keith Jones who milked their properties for all they were worth, thereby depriving tenants of the basic amenities they were paying their good money for. Did Jones realize how foolish he'd been? Dissatisfied tenants always moved. Couldn't he see that his neglect had lowered his rents and caused his high vacancy rate?

Fools like him deserved to go bankrupt. Not that

they ever blamed themselves. No doubt Jones saw her as the villain in this foreclosure.

Her heart hardened as she viewed the sagging gutters at the roofline and the many huge potholes in the asphalt parking lot. Paint peeled from wooden facings. This project was in even worse shape than his other properties. She wished Jones hadn't fallen behind on his notes, so she wouldn't have to foreclose next week and sink her good money after his bad or, worse, bulldoze the buildings. Not that his properties weren't prime locations.

How she pitied poor people who had to live in buildings like these. Her green eyes narrowed on a crack that ran from the top of one building, all the way down to a scraggly bush and to—

To two filthy, unlaced athletic shoes sticking out from the dense foliage. The toes were glued together in a raptly tense, pigeon-toed position. The ragged cuffs of a pair of equally filthy jeans were all that was visible of the slim little boy.

Kate softened inwardly. She wanted people to believe she was a cool, controlled, brilliant businesswoman who gloried in her independence and glamorous single life, who gloried in the local fame she had achieved through her weekly column. She wanted them to think that she was just like her controlled, highly disciplined father who had never loved another human being in his life, that her sole passion was enlarging the Karlington empire, just as his had been. In truth, she wished she *was* like that. She wanted to be as invulnerable to hurt as he had been, but there had always been in her that secret weakness, that cra-

ven, instinctive yearning for any scrap of tenderness
and love.

When she was growing up, her father had never
allowed her to have a pet or friends. Later, after she'd
run away to her aunt Mathilde's, he'd coldly refused
to take Kate back. Instead, he'd sent her to schools
as far away as possible, rarely allowing her to come
home for holidays. So she had grown up lonely. Feeling isolated and rejected even after she'd obtained
several degrees, she had fallen for the first man who
had pretended he loved her. Not that the illusion had
lasted long, for her father had ruthlessly exposed all
of Edwin's failings and his true motivations in marrying her. Edwin had had other women all along. He
had married her for the Karlington money; he had
never loved her.

After he'd left her, she'd discovered she was pregnant. When she told him, he'd been coldly indifferent.
During those brief first months of her pregnancy,
she'd imagined that at last she would have someone
she could love and who would love her. Then, at the
end of her fifth month, she had miscarried.

The baby's memorial service had seemed the end
of everything. It had taken her a long time to recover.
Outwardly she seemed fine. Inwardly the wounds
sometimes felt as raw as ever.

Her failed marriage had made Kate wary of men,
but even though the loss of her baby had hurt far
more, even though she didn't trust herself with men,
she secretly longed to try to have another child. And
it seemed that the closer she got to her thirtieth birthday, the stronger the instinctive urge to be a mother

became. She couldn't walk through Neiman's or Saks without staring at the children's clothes in frustration and wishing she had a little girl or a little boy of her own to buy something cute for. She would remember the months of joy when she had planned for the birth of her baby, and all the darling things she had bought. Only to have to pack them away.

Was she really doomed to spend her whole life alone?

The ragtag boy was so quiet and still, for a second she was terrified he'd been hit by a car and crawled out of the street to die. Then she heard a page flip and an awestruck exclamation.

"Golly-damn-bongo!"

She sank down beside him, sighing in relief and in shock at his language, for never having had them, she idealized children. "Hello there," she said softly.

He started guiltily, scrambling out from under the bush, intending to run.

Until she grabbed him gently but firmly by the collar.

Despite his filthy T-shirt and ragged jeans, he was beautiful. He had dark curly hair and dark flashing eyes. "I didn't mean to scare you," she said, again in her gentlest tone.

"I wasn't scared. I ain't some sissy," he said in a rough, put-on, big-boy voice.

"*Am not,*" she corrected. "Of course you're not. But what were you doing under there?"

He thrust back his chin and glued his dark rebellious eyes to a distant spot behind her. "Just readin'," he mumbled, reddening.

"Must be good. Can I see—"

"No!"

Her brows arched.

"I mean it's nothing you'd be interested in—ma'am," he said more politely.

When she reached down for the magazine, he lunged to grab it.

Then the wind caught the sexy centerfold, and it fluttered like a flag. The boy cried out in acute dismay, springing for the slick, greasily thumbed thing.

But she was quicker.

"Oh, my," she gasped, shocked as she got an eyeful of bulging bosom and pink fanny.

The little scamp would have run, but she clung to his collar.

The young woman who adorned the centerfold was amazingly proportioned. *Golly-damn-bongo is right,* Kate thought with a smile, and then was horrified that she could be amused. Boy and woman blushed as they studied the centerfold with equal fascination until she remembered herself and snapped it out of his line of vision.

Kate found the picture deeply degrading to all women on principle. No wonder little boys grew into men seeing women as nothing more than sex objects. No wonder rich men thought women could be bought. Not just rich men. She remembered the way Edwin had used the Karlington money to attract younger women.

"Where did you get this, young man?"

"Found it."

"Where?"

"Dunno."

"You do, too!" She shook him slightly.

"Under a bed. I was cleaning out an apartment for my father...picking up trash...."

"Where is your mother?"

"Dead."

The word wrenched her because of her own lonely, motherless childhood and her hard, rejecting father.

"She died three years ago when I was only six." He lowered his head.

Kate had been about the same age when her own mother died. If this beautiful child were hers, Kate would never have set him to clean some trashy apartment.

"Where's your father?"

"Doing the yard."

Kate frowned. So his father was the yardman. It surprised her that Jones, who was so close with his money when it came to paint, lumber and asphalt, would spend a cent on grass. She guessed that even he had some standards—low as they were.

"Don't tell on me," the boy pleaded in a pitiful voice. "Dad's not feeling too good and he gets mad when I slack off."

She'd always been terrified of her father, too. "Is he sick?"

"Hung over."

Kate's eyes narrowed. There was ice suddenly, on her forehead, icy indignant rage spreading from the nape of her neck down her spine. Why had this wonderful little angel been given to some alcoholic brutish laborer who would neglect him, a man who was obviously lousy at his job…when she—

"I won't let him hurt you," she said protectively as she led the child into the courtyard.

She saw the ax and the chain saw first; and then the wheelbarrow and the mower and the tangled mountain of clippings the dark giant had piled beside him.

When she walked briskly up to him, he ignored her and continued to rip weeds from the flower bed.

He wasn't lazy.

Kate admired energy in people, especially when they applied it to something constructive. She didn't have a single employee who worked so ferociously as this brute.

She saw him well for the first time.

Rivulets of steamy sweat raced down the man's neck and his arms. She licked her lips. Just for a second before she caught herself, she felt a funny feeling start in the pit of her stomach at the sight of so much hard male muscle. She, who had schooled herself never to look at men, couldn't be fascinated by this man's flexing, bronze biceps.

She tried to swallow but couldn't. She looked away instead. "Hello," she said, intending her firmest, no-nonsense tone, only to be furious when her voice sounded vulnerable and shaky—almost sexy.

She didn't want to like him.

Her experiences with men had taught her they came in two categories. Rich men of her own class were too often like her father—selfish to the core. When they wanted to get rid of a child, they paid someone to take care of it. When they wanted a woman's body, they found her price. Such men didn't have to give emotionally of themselves. All her father had ever given her were things. When she was a teenager and had asked him to take her places, he'd had a fancy convertible delivered to her school.

Poorer men worshiped money as ardently as rich ones because they believed it was magic. She had learned that from Edwin, her ex-husband, who had pretended he'd loved her when all he'd ever wanted was her money.

"I—I said hello," Kate repeated, forcing herself to look at the man again. Dear God. Her voice came out even huskier than before.

He went still, as if the raspy sound had electrified him.

Her gaze fixed on his rigid brown arms. She felt her own muscles go as tense as his. It was as if she were in tune with this scowling brute. Which was ridiculous.

Slowly he brushed the dirt from his fingers and rose angrily to his full height.

Clearly he didn't want to be interrupted.

He was very, very tall. Well over six feet.

She liked tall.

No, she didn't!

He was a sleek-muscled, black-haired, deplorably handsome Adonis, who was so disgustingly male and virile that her womb ached with sudden awareness of the profound loneliness of her life. Despite the differences she imagined between herself and him—class, education, ambition, the zillion cultural refinements she possessed and he could not possibly—his hot, faintly insolent gaze lit that spark of deep feminine yearning.

He was as set on disliking her as she was on him. But for an infinitesimal moment as his smoldering black eyes slid from her face down her body, she knew that on some primitive level she wanted to devour him in the same hideous, stripping way his gaze was so hatefully devouring her.

No… She—she, cool, collected Kate Karlington, who had schooled herself to turn up her nose at the advances of far more eligible bachelors, wouldn't allow herself to have the hots for this sulky, muscle-bound Neanderthal.

Her blood burned through her like fire anyway. Suddenly she felt so dizzy, she was afraid she might actually faint.

"What's the matter?" he demanded in a harsh baritone that was absolutely beautiful.

"I—I'm fine.…"

"You're shaking like a leaf."

"Allergies," she lied.

"Right," he muttered in that velvety, deeply unsettling tone.

He was smarter than she'd thought. She had to make her point and escape him. "I—I found your son in the parking lot—reading.…"

The brute's dazzling smile made her whole body tighten. Why did his rugged masculine face have to be carved in such appealingly tough lines? He had a strong jaw, a straight nose. Spiked black lashes set off his bold angry eyes. She noticed the tiny lines at the corners of those dark eyes that seemed so intelligent—silent testimony that when he wasn't sulking, he had a sense of humor.

"Bobby Lee reading?" His wicked smile broadened. "That's a new one."

She caught the smell of his beery breath, and some stronger, sweaty male scent that was not altogether displeasing as he ruffled his son's black hair with brutish pride. When the beast's gaze raked her with scathing intent, she took a hesitant step backward before she reminded herself of her mission.

"Don't you even care what he was reading?" she demanded.

Her high-and-mighty tone brought a swift scowl.

"I care," he said with soft menace. "Show me."

"Here!" She thrust the magazine forward.

Roughly he yanked it from her and studied the nude centerfold with an embarrassing avidity.

Kate colored when his black eyes flicked back from the lush splendor of the naked girl to trail down her own body.

As if to compare her to—

His look shamed her to the core.

She wanted to run, to die.

He rolled the magazine up and stuffed it into the back pocket of his jeans. Then he knelt to his son's level and said, "We'll take this up again tonight when we're alone…and have a man-to-man talk. For now, get back to number 20 and clean it up—on the double. Or I'll give you an extra hour of pulling weeds."

The kid bolted like a streak of lightning.

"The threat of weed pulling always gets him going,'' the Neanderthal muttered with a grim smile, his gaze following the running child and his flapping shoestrings.

She was furious. ''Is that all you intend to do?'' She curled her long nails into her palms. ''What kind of father are you? You find your son reading filth, and…and you don't even care.''

The man's eyes returned to her slowly. ''He's my kid—not yours! And I'm a helluva lot more concerned about his habit of shirking work than the fact that he has a boy's natural interest in sex.''

''A boy's natural interest? Is that what you call it? Why am I surprised that someone like you would be more concerned with driving a child, too young to work, to do your job than with his morals? You probably don't even know what morals are. You probably don't care that he cusses, either.''

The man's hard features went tighter. ''Hey— you're way out of line, lady. Who the hell do you think you are, coming here, criticizing the way I raise my child? All boys do some cussing and looking at pictures like that when they get the chance.''

As he moved toward her, she shrank from him. To her horror, her shoulders hit cool pink bricks, and she realized he had her cornered against a cracked, mildewed wall. He leaned into her, his huge body cutting her off from freedom.

''Where were you raised—a convent?''

She whitened. He was closer to the truth than he knew.

''It's plain as day you have problems you can't deal with, lady. You're probably so damn rich, you never worked an honest day in your life. You just go out and buy what you want or use your money to take what you want. You probably think you're too good to get dirty and sweaty. Well, I started working younger than him. Work won't hurt him. Neither will that magazine.''

''Why did I ever think I could talk to you?'' She started to push past him, but he brought his arms up beside her, blocking her escape.

''And another thing, lady—the fact that I'm not horrified by Bobby Lee's interest in sex has nothing to do with my morals, which I probably have way more of than you do.

''I let you butt your long, uptight nose into my life just for the fun of it. But you got me all stirred up and curious. Why the hell is a beautiful woman like yourself so scared of sex when it's the best thing this life has to offer?''

''A man…like you…would think that.''

''Most of the women I've known would agree.''

''Only the worst kind of woman would consort with someone as low as you.''

''I should break your snotty little neck for that.''

''Violence…from a man like you wouldn't surprise me, either.''

He took a deep calming breath. ''I don't know why I give a damn what you think, but, for the record, I'm not some kind of savage where women are concerned. I married my high school sweetheart. And I would have been faithful to her till I died if she hadn't died first.'' His voice broke, and he looked away, his shattered face darker and angrier than ever as if he despised himself for revealing anything so personal to her.

She saw the wild grief in his ravaged eyes and forgot her terror of him.

There was a long awkward moment. She felt drawn to him because she instinctively knew that his grief and loneliness were every bit as terrible as her own.

On some crazy, overwrought impulse, she gently touched his arm, her soft fingertips sliding comfortingly along his hard, hot muscles. Flesh to flesh. Heart to heart. Woman to man.

The touch of him compelled her. For one long instant, she felt the most powerful, uncanny connection to him she had ever felt to anyone.

Then he jerked his arm away. "Don't touch me! Don't you ever put your lily-white hands on me again," he roared.

"I—I didn't mean to! I must have been crazy to! It…it was an accident!"

"Good!"

"Just get out of my way, and I'll go," she said primly.

"Not till you tell me what you're doing on Jones property. My, er, boss gave me instructions about a certain woman—Karlington. He told me to call the cops if she came around."

"I'm not her!"

"She's got red hair."

Her eyes widened, and he laughed at her fear.

"If you don't let me go, I'll scream."

"Would you really?"

She tried to nod, but the muscles in her neck felt frozen.

"I could stop you from that, you know."

But instead of pressing his physical advantage, he lifted his arms, and she moved away from the wall, away from him, only to trip over his wheelbarrow and cry out furiously.

When he started toward her, she held up her hands. "No— Don't come near me! I can get up by myself." She brushed frantically at the loose dirt and grass on her linen slacks.

"You didn't tell me what you're doing here," he demanded.

"I—I was looking for an apartment."

"Like hell." His words were harsh. "This isn't exactly your kind of neighborhood."

"N-not for myself," she improvised wildly. "For someone who...who works for me."

"Oh, right. Some lowlife like me. Lady Bountiful apartment hunting for her...her yardman, maybe? Why is that such a hard one to swallow?" He flashed that cynical smile of his again and dug in his pocket.

He knew she was lying, and for some idiotic reason she felt ashamed that he thought she was a snob.

While his fingers moved beneath the denim, her gaze flicked to his powerful body.

The bronzed muscular perfection of his lean frame drew her. For no reason at all, she thought of her big double bed and how empty and cold it felt every night.

She looked breathlessly away, but not before his dark gaze swung to her, and she felt the leap of some wild charge between them. He was as turned on by her as she was by him.

She shuddered, and he scowled. She realized a man like him might have taken her touching his arm as an invitation to do anything; he was so strong, she couldn't have stopped him. She was lucky he disliked her and had jerked away from her.

She didn't feel lucky. She felt lonely.

So lonely.

Dear God. She wanted to run, to forget Keith Jones and his deplorable properties and his even more deplorable employee.

But the brown hand had closed over the object it had been digging for. Carelessly, the yardman pulled his hand from his pocket and tossed her a shiny key.

His toss was on. But she was so upset, her catch was off. As she leaned down to pick it up, she was aware of his bold eyes on her.

"Number 15 is empty and ready to rent," he said casually in that harsh, but oh-so-compelling voice. "I cleaned it and repaired the appliances myself, and I could give you a personal tour. I'm good with my hands." He paused. Maybe to let that last sentence sink in and torment her. "Good at fixing things, I mean. There's a kitchen, a living room, a bath. And, of course, a bedroom." He drawled that last word ever so suggestively. "Or you can look it over yourself."

She gasped in relief. "I—I'll look it over on my own."

"Independent lady…"

"Bingo."

"You can leave the key in the door. I'll be here…if you need me.… For anything.''

She felt hot and weak. He was horrible. He seemed to hate her, and yet he seemed to find some savage delight in tormenting her, too. Why did some terrible wanton weakness make her want to ask him to show her the apartment after all?

No.…

When she whirled away from him, she thought she heard him chuckle darkly.

But when she turned back, he scowled at her obligingly.

Damn the man.

Chapter Three

Kate stood frozen in the doorway of number 15, wanting to leave but not wanting to risk more attention from the insolent yardman, who was now mowing the courtyard.

So she lingered in that shadowy entrance—trapped by her ridiculous fear of a man who was so far beneath her, she should never have noticed him in the first place. Nevertheless, she had to admit to a grudging admiration for him, at least for his work. Menial though some might believe it, he obviously took pride in it.

The apartment was immaculate. Not only did all the ancient appliances sparkle, they worked. Maybe his boss wasn't so bad after all. Maybe Jones did try to offer decent housing. Maybe he just couldn't afford to paint the outside.

Since her gaze was glued to the man's broad back, she saw the splash from the swimming pool only out of the corner of her eye. But she panicked when she realized that Bobby Lee, who had been playing by the pool only a few seconds before, had vanished.

As she raced for the pool, she had no way of knowing whether or not he could swim. Then she saw a sickening dark shape with flailing legs on the bottom of the deep end.

Rushing through the chain-link gate, she sprang toward the pool, but as she dove, the slim heel of her Italian sandal snagged in a crack in the cement. She pitched wildly off balance, her head striking the hard tile edge of the pool. Her body slid into the water just as the kid's curly black head broke the aqua surface.

When Kate woke up, her throat and nasal passages burned with every breath. She groaned as she felt large hands gently probing her damp hair. Then the brutal fingertips dug too deeply into the gash in her scalp, and her eyes snapped open.

"Ouch!"

For an instant she didn't recognize the swarthy hard face so close to hers. Then the dark eyes flashed, and the man smiled sardonically as if he didn't respect her much.

And she knew who he was.

Confused, she glanced wildly past him and saw scuffed black work boots tossed in a corner, a masculine tie looped carelessly over a doorknob and a denim work shirt draped over a dresser that was littered with magazines and newspapers and a tattered paperback copy of *The Fatal Skin* by Honoré de Balzac.

He wasn't neat. Which didn't surprise her.

But he read. Which did.

"Where am I?" she demanded even as she saw that the insolent brute had taken advantage of the situation and maneuvered her into his bedroom.

"My bed," he replied, his husky voice low and somehow dangerous.

She pushed his hands away furiously.

"As if I couldn't figure that out! I meant why am I here? How did I get here?" she squeaked shrilly, struggling to sit up.

"I wouldn't sit up if I were you," he advised. "Take it easy. You've had a blow to the head. Not that it seems to have improved your disposition. On the contrary—"

"It'll take more than a blow to my head to keep me in your bed!"

But as she spoke, the crisp cotton sheet and heavy blankets sliding downward against her cool skin almost exposed a bare breast. Blushing, she grabbed at the sheet, conscious of a new horror and an excellent reason for staying right where she was.

Beneath his sheets and blankets, she was stark naked.

She froze, her hands groping wildly over her body just to make sure while his gleaming dark eyes told her he was enjoying her discomfiture immensely.

"You…you stripped me," she whispered, yanking his sheet to her chin and holding it there primly.

His loathsome smile broadened. "Doctor's orders."

A dozen hot nerves were quivering in her temple. "I'll bet!" She was about to explode. Instead she stopped herself and sucked in her breath.

"You were soaking wet. Doc said the first thing to do was make sure you were dry and warm. You see, you hit your head on the pool edge and fell in—unconscious."

"And you saved me?"

"You got it, baby. I'm your hero. I pulled you out

of the pool and called a doctor. Which makes me your Sir Lance in shining armor.''

He smiled as if he was loving every minute of this!

She felt a killing rage and an unendurable shame. ''Not in a million lifetimes.'' Just the thought that he was gloating over having seen her without a stitch on made her cheeks burn.

''And where are my clothes?''

His black eyes went cold. ''I bet Bobby Lee you'd act high and mighty and refuse to thank us.''

She clamped her lips together in a stubborn line. Gratitude was the last thing she felt. Still, he did have her trapped…and in his bed. ''Thank you—for saving me,'' she muttered grudgingly. ''Now…if…if you would…please…please…just get my clothes, I'll dress and go.''

''Relax.'' His avid attention focused on her hot face. ''You're not leaving till the doctor gets here and says you can.''

''I—I'm sure…I've caused you enough trouble.''

''Don't worry about it,'' he murmured ruthlessly. ''I knew you were trouble the minute I set eyes on you. Besides I've enjoyed…getting to know you better.''

Inwardly she was seething—and he knew it. His gorgeous mouth was twitching, which meant he loved it. Outwardly she struggled to act calm and dignified. ''Look, you may be used to situations like this—''

''Why do I have the feeling you're about to hurt my feelings by attacking my morals again?'' he taunted softly.

"Well, a man like you probably has strange naked women in his bed all the time—"

"Right! A man like me.... So, we're back to me being a lowlife, are we? No one has been in my bed...since my wife died. And you, my holier-than-thou Karlington witch, are no stranger to me. If I did want a woman, you're the very last I'd choose—to have naked in my bed." He had drawled her name very softly, very nastily.

She bristled even as his frigid tone sent a chill down her spine. "How do you know my name?"

"When you were out cold, I told Bobby Lee to look in your purse for your driver's license."

He was lying. She could feel it.

"Bobby Lee's okay, then?" she asked weakly.

"He was diving for a toy car. He's fine."

"You should have been watching him."

The man's features were half in shadow, the hard angular planes revealing little. "Hey, you're the last person I'd let tell me what I should and shouldn't do. You're the fool who would have drowned if I hadn't saved you."

"Well, if you'll just get my clothes, I'll cause you no further trouble."

"No way do I believe that.... Not that I'll give you your clothes...."

Her pulse began to throb unevenly.

"Don't worry—I have no designs on your body, charming though it is," he said bluntly. "But you're staying till the doctor says you can go. You see, Miss Karlington, my boss told me you were repossessing everything he owns. He ordered me not to allow you to set foot on his property till you got title. He'll fire me for sure if he finds out I let you snoop around here and then you nearly drowned in his pool—because of my kid.''

''I hope you do get fired. I hope you starve.''

Low, harsh laughter came from his throat. ''Because you've always been so rich, you've never had it tough,'' he murmured tightly. ''You wouldn't mind Bobby Lee losing his home.''

''I—I don't want to hurt Bobby Lee. Only you—because—''

''Because I didn't pussyfoot around someone as high and mighty as you think you are,'' he ground out. ''Because I was afraid you'd go into shock and I had the audacity to undress you when you were shivering and unconscious. Honey, you were out cold, and your skin was like ice.''

She was still stuck on the word *honey,* savoring it, hating him for saying it in that cynical and yet deeply caressing tone that made her feel very feminine and cherished even as it turned her blood to molten fire.

''If you get me fired, Bobby Lee'll pay, too. What happens to me, happens to him. The question is, are you as cold and ruthless as Jones says you are?''

''Oh, all right. I'll see your doctor,'' she snapped, not answering his question because for some reason she didn't want to admit she was probably worse than Jones said she was.

His eyebrows arched nastily.

''I'm staying for Bobby Lee's sake! Not yours. And I won't say a thing to Jones to get you in trouble even though you're insolent…and…arrogant. Even though you don't know your…your place.''

"Which is light years socially beneath your brightly shining star?'' he added shortly.

"You said it, buster. I'll even pay for the doctor. There's a fifty in my purse—''

"I'll pay,'' he growled.

"Oh, don't be so proud! You can't possibly afford—''

"Jones'll reimburse me. The last thing he'd want is *your* money.''

"You make it sound as if he hates me.'' It irritated her that Jones went around running her down to her future employees.

"Yeah. Do you blame him?'' Flushing darkly, the brute leaned closer, and a shiver of alarm darted through her. "But then, Jones hasn't had the pleasure of getting to know you personally—on the intimate level that I have.''

Kate tried to tell herself that he was crude and uneducated and insolent, that she hated the idea of such a man's dark callused hands on her skin, of his bold eyes burning now with memories of her naked body. But as his gaze devoured her lips, and his mouth came nearer, a violent quiver went hotly through her, and without fully realizing what she did, she closed her eyes and pursed her lips almost expectantly.

If he'd been as tempted to kiss her as she'd been to let him, he mastered the impulse. Instead of his warm mouth on hers, she felt a draft of cool air and heard his raspy chuckle as the door swung open.

When her eyes flew open again, the Balzac novel was gone and a tanned hand was pulling the door shut.

Monday morning, Kate's temple still ached as she flicked on the lights of her darkened office and walked briskly to her desk with her heavy briefcase. She opened her crisp beige drapes, and hazy sunlight flooded her opulent, immaculate office.

She wore a starched white cotton blouse and a perfectly pressed denim skirt. Her hair was pulled straight back from her face and secured tightly in a big white clip.

For a long moment she stared out the ceiling-to-floor windows at the bustling city wrapped in smog. She felt strangely restless and lonelier than ever before, cut off from that world of ordinary people who had families and lovers and children.

Her father had warned her she would be alone at the top, that her money would set her apart, that she could trust in nothing and in no one except herself; that men would want her only for her power or for her fortune, that she would have to learn to make men her tools, her serfs, and not become theirs.

Own or be owned. Control or be controlled. Those were her father's rules. He said there was no such thing as a power vacuum. Either you were in charge or you were exploited.

Once she had not wanted to believe that, and she had been naively loving. But Edwin's cruel betrayal had taught her that her father was right. Never had she felt more exploited than when she'd lain in the hospital after her miscarriage and her father had coldly informed her by phone how much he'd paid in the divorce settlement to be rid of Edwin.

She had asked her father, "Did you tell him I lost the baby?"

"You little fool... Yes."

And when Edwin had not bothered to come to the baby's memorial service, her heart had hardened. Not only toward him, but toward all men.

Kate came back to the present.

She turned her back on the window and sat down, a tiny solitary figure dwarfed by her immense office. With a shaking hand she withdrew the thick, perfectly organized Jones file from her briefcase and thumbed through the neat pages.

Involuntarily her thoughts turned to her accident Saturday and to that humiliating encounter with Jones's insolent yardman and to his friend, the helpful Dr. Sager. When she took over the Jones properties, she would have that rude, impossible handyman fired. Then she remembered Bobby Lee and realized that much as she hated helping the father, she would have to arrange for one of her friends to hire him for the sake of his child. She had seen the man's work and could personally recommend him. Even though she knew that, professionally, she was an idiot to let go of someone so good, she was too afraid of seeing him again.

Because she had dreamed of him.

Because she had longed for him even though she knew he hated her, and she hated him.

She had puttered about her apartment Sunday, going through the motions of neatening and straightening drawers and closets that had already been perfect. She had felt edgy and restless and lonely, which she, independent Kate Karlington, resented because she believed she didn't need a man for anything.

Not true. Men had one use for which there was no good substitute. She thought of how warm the yard-man's hard arm had felt beneath her fingers before he had jerked away from her.

Her thoughts strayed beyond sex. More than anything in the world, Kate wanted a child. She wanted someone to love, someone who would love her. But she was old enough to have come to terms with some other facts about herself and her beliefs. Her cruel experiences had taught her to distrust herself with men; she didn't want to risk another failed marriage.

She remembered how joyous, how filled with hope she'd felt when she'd been pregnant. The motherhood angle seemed a more enduring love bond.

There should be some sort of painless baby machine a mature woman such as herself could use to get pregnant.

A baby machine…

In spite of herself, Kate smiled faintly and closed her eyes, trying to imagine one. It should be a robot with steel arms and bright lights for eyes. The procedure to get pregnant would have to be painless and, of course, it wouldn't be fraught with emotional complications. But neither the vision nor the procedure would take shape in her mind. Instead she imagined an angry man whose powerful body seemed made of melted bronze, whose raven-black hair was glossily curled, whose cruel white smile made her shiver as he pulled her naked body beneath his onto a soft bed of tangled white sheets.

Softly she touched her breasts through her starched cotton shirt, and unbidden came the forbidden memory of the yardman's insolent black eyes moving lingeringly over her body, of the molten electricity that had raced through her every time he'd looked at her even when she'd known he disliked her. She remembered his breath, warm and beery smelling, and yet earthily pleasant; she remembered his desperate pain when he'd mentioned the death of his wife. And she remembered his dear, motherless little boy. For all their differences, she sensed the man was as lonely as she was. More than anything she wanted to see the man and his beautiful little boy again.

She tried to imagine the man, dressed in a three-piece suit, with an education as fancy as hers. Fortunately, Kate's ridiculous daydreams were shattered when her large polished mahogany door was pushed open by her secretary. Esther Ayers rushed in clutching her baby daughter, Hannah, in one arm and a bottle of juice and a stack of legal papers in the other.

"Sorry, Kate, but Mom had to go to the dentist, so I had to bring Hannah in for an hour or so. You see, yesterday we took Mother to a restaurant for Mothers' Day after church. Mother shattered a molar when she bit into an oyster."

Mother's Day—Kate ignored her own pain as she remembered going to her own mother's grave and then to the grave of her baby with a bouquet of daisies. She had never gotten to celebrate a single

Mother's Day with her mother. She herself would probably never really be a mother.

She got up slowly and held out her arms to the golden two-year-old. With a giggle, Hannah sprang into them.

Esther set the papers on her desk. "These have to be signed so they can go out—today."

"You know I love for you to bring Hannah," Kate said softly. She touched her forehead to the child's and then caressed her golden ringlets. "Hello, there, my beautiful darling. Now how many piggies—"

"Fingas, Kate! Toes! Not piggies!" Hannah squealed, hiding her eyes bashfully.

"Your Mr. Jones has been calling all morning demanding to see you," Esther said.

"My lawyers have advised against such a meeting till the day of the foreclosure."

"You should try telling him that."

The phone rang again.

"That's probably him," Esther said.

Esther was about to pick up the phone, but Kate lifted the receiver herself, knowing Esther really wasn't tough enough to handle certain macho, overbearing types. Kate knelt so Hannah could get down to explore.

"Karlington Enterprises. Miss Karlington's office," Kate said smoothly, pretending to be her secretary.

"Honey, put the dragon lady through, and I swear I'll take you to the fanciest lunch Houston can offer."

Bribery. Kate frowned, even though she knew Esther was too loyal to ever go out with him.

"I'm so sorry. Miss Karlington has someone in her office at the moment, sir," Kate said frostily. Which wasn't exactly a lie.

"Good! She's there! I'll be right over."

"No, I don't want—! I mean *her* lawyers have advised her not to see—"

"Honey, the trouble with this damned country is the lawyers are running it."

"She's too busy to see you. Besides, you're the last man she wants to see."

"Then why did she come snooping around my property Saturday? You tell her that one of my people says she took off her clothes, hopped in his bed and sexually harassed him. Those are some pretty serious charges. I try to run a moral establishment."

"He what? I tell you Ms. Karlington did no such thing! He stripped her—"

Kate broke off, her skin flaming as Esther's curious gaze rose to hers.

"She tried to seduce him into kissing—"

Frantically Kate waved her curious secretary out of the room.

"She most certainly did not!"

"I'm surprised Miss Karlington would keep her secretary so well-informed about such activities—"

Kate's voice was steel. "This is Kate Karlington, Mr. Jones."

"I knew it all the time."

"And I don't want to see you."

"Oh, but you do," he said very softly. "Every bit as much as I want to see you. Women have chased me all my life. From my yardman's description of you, I doubt you'll be any exception. I'm looking forward to meeting you—in the flesh.''

"You are as impossible as that horrible man who works for you."

"He and I have a great deal in common."

"I wouldn't brag about it if I were you."

"Funny, but he told me that under different circumstances, you two could have hit it off."

"He what?'' she screamed.

When he didn't answer, she realized he'd hung up.

Dear God! He was probably on his way over.

Chapter Four

"I-cream! I-cream!" Hannah leaned forward and pointed to the giant poster of a pink cow licking the top of a huge double-dip parfait coated in chocolate syrup and peanuts. Then Hannah turned her attention back to the man behind the black-and-white-tiled counter who was digging in a huge ice-cream carton for a ball of vanilla.

"I want my *big* i-cream!"

"He's making it, Hannah darling. Just as fast as he can," Kate said soothingly.

"Zakly like the picture?"

"Exactly, precious."

As soon as Kate had hung up from speaking to Jim Keith Jones, Hannah had insisted on being taken downstairs to the ice-cream parlor, which was on the street level. Such trips had become ritual affairs whenever Esther brought her daughter to the office, and today Kate had been only too happy to leave Esther to deal with the troublesome Mr. Jones.

The glass door of the shop suddenly swung open, and a familiar-looking black-haired little boy burst inside and dashed to the counter. "Dad, can I have one of those—" He pointed to the same poster that had caught Hannah's attention.

Hannah put her thumb in her mouth and chewed

on it, regarding the interloper curiously while the door was opened slowly and closed again.

"Sure, son. Whatever you want," came the deep velvet tones of an unforgettable, masculine baritone. Kate turned around wildly. The bold blaze of devil-black eyes stared holes through her.

Her heart began to hammer in a painful rush.

"Why, if it isn't the beautiful witch Karlington," came the smooth whisper of the yardman Kate would have given anything to avoid. He didn't look the least bit surprised to see her. Nor the least bit flustered.

Kate clutched the counter for support as the man behind it placed a cherry on top of Hannah's magnificent, double-dip parfait. "There you go, miss—"

"It's not as big as the picture," Hannah cried in dismay.

The yardman smiled grimly. "Most things men do don't live up to a woman's expectations. Not that I've had many complaints from women."

Kate ignored the plastic cup and the towering parfait in the outstretched hand and whirled angrily to stare at the tall man now striding toward her.

He had talked to his boss.

She was about to tell him he was the most conceited blabbermouth she had ever met, but she stopped short. He no longer looked at all like a yardman. Someone with impeccable taste had put him in an elegant black three-piece suit, and he looked even better in it than she'd imagined he would.

No longer did he seem such a lesser being—a ghetto-toughened, uneducated hunk fit only to do menial work. No, this man could fit as easily into her elegant world as he could a darker, more dangerous one. Despite his rough edges, there was the unmistakable aura of keen-minded power about him, as if he was as ruthlessly used to commanding others as she.

Why did the image of that tattered novel by Balzac flash in her mind?

"What a coincidence," he purred raspily, "our meeting again." He was smiling in that grim, bold way that so unnerved Kate because she sensed that their meeting here was no coincidence. He had deliberately hunted her down for some purpose of his own.

She flashed him a tight smile of dismissal and picked up Hannah's parfait.

"Thanks for telling your boss what happened! Did he send you over to do his dirty work?" she whispered.

"Oh, this was my brainchild," he replied while his son ordered a parfait.

"Why?"

"Would you believe I was worried about you and wanted to make sure you were okay?"

"No!"

"Right." His voice was both soft and deep, but he didn't smile. "And you probably intend to hold what happened Saturday against me forever."

"You and I are hardly going to have a forever."

"I'm truly glad you're better."

She couldn't believe it when he touched her injured temple very gently, smoothing her red hair away from her face. "We may be more involved than you think."

"I-cream! I-cream!" Hannah cried impatiently. "Melting!"

"Sorry, darling." Kate turned her back on the yardman and carried Hannah to the nearest booth, placing the mountain of ice cream in front of her, and sitting opposite the child so she could help her.

The yardman handed his son a five-dollar bill, and, without asking if he could join Kate, pulled up a tiny pink stool that was much too small for him and thrust his long legs on either side of it. Hannah had eaten only one bite, but ice cream was already dripping over the plastic sides of her cup and down her chin. Nevertheless, she smiled flirtatiously at the handsome man she took to be her new admirer.

The elegant yardman smiled back at her, picked up a napkin and wiped her small face with a fatherly, well-practiced expertise.

The ogre's roughly carved features were almost sweet as he dealt with Hannah.

"You have a beautiful little girl, Mrs. Karlington— underneath the chocolate syrup," he said.

"It's Miss—"

"Right. I think my boss read somewhere that your husband ran off with a younger woman."

"And I divorced him and took my maiden name back. And Hannah's—not my daughter, either."

The yardman's hard black eyes met Kate's, and she realized he'd caught the pain in her voice.

"But you wish she was," he said quietly.

"Yes," Kate admitted, unnerved that he seemed to understand her on a soul-deep level.

"Maybe you wouldn't like a kid any more than a

husband if you were stuck cleaning up chocolate twenty-four hours a day."

"You're wrong. Very, very wrong." Kate frowned.

Bobby Lee joined them, sitting on a stool across from Hannah.

"Why did you really come here?" Kate asked the yardman.

"I told you—to make sure you're okay."

"I'm okay. So you can go. Unless you have some other reason—"

"As a matter of fact I do."

"I'm all ears."

"Since you're going to buy the Jones properties, and I...I work for Jones, I thought maybe I should ask what you intend to do about his people. I mean the little guys...like me."

"I intend to keep most of his people," she hedged, not wanting to admit that she had decided to terminate him.

"That's a relief."

She flushed guiltily.

His face grew hard. "And what about me? Are you going to toss me out into the cold?"

Again he seemed to have read her mind.

Something inside her froze. "Each case will be judged individually," she whispered, turning pale.

"I'm afraid I made a very bad impression."

"Yes."

"I did so deliberately."

"Why did you have to tell your boss everything that happened?"

"He and I are very close."

He took her hand, and the shock of his touch was electric. She tried to draw back, but he held on to her slim fingers tightly.

"W-what do you think you're doing?" she managed to ask.

"Now, this isn't an apology. It's an explanation. I don't like people who walk over other people. Who use their money to buy lawyers and steal legally. I see them as bullies." His hard voice softened. "Even when they are very beautiful."

The warmth in his eyes made her shiver. "I can see Jones has been talking to you out of hand. If your boss has problems, it has nothing to do with me. It's due to his own ineptness."

His fingers tightened on hers. His hard mouth thinned, but he did not defend his boss. "Has your own life gone perfectly? Have you never made a mistake that you deeply regret?"

She stared at him in silence, too aware of her small hand locked in his larger one. Too aware of his heat, his power, his charisma. His immense frame seemed to shrink the size of the booth, to overwhelm her.

"You can work for me—for double what Jones paid you," she said on a desperate note.

His mouth twisted. "You're more generous than you know. But I won't hold you to that."

Hannah looked up and declared proudly, "I'm tru." She lifted her golden head out of the ice-cream dish, her chin and nose dripping with chocolate syrup and vanilla ice cream.

And one glance at her brought the adult conversation to an abrupt end.

* * *

Ten minutes later, when Jim Keith strode into Kate's outer office and lavish waiting room, Hannah giggled flirtatiously at him. He smiled back at her on his way past Esther, who was talking on the phone at her desk.

"Wait for me here, Bobby Lee," Jim Keith commanded, pointing to a chair near Hannah.

Bobby Lee ran over to play with the little girl. Jim Keith was about to push open the massive mahogany door that led to Kate's office, when Esther called to him frantically.

"Sir? Sir, do you have an appointment?"

"Your boss is expecting me."

Esther studied her appointment book. "I don't see a ten forty-five."

Jim Keith moved swiftly to her desk, leaned down, and scribbled his name. When he finished, huge, bold black scrawl filled the entire page. "Now you do. We've talked on the phone."

"Jones?" Esther squeaked, deciphering the scribble. Then her big eyes traveled slowly from her book up the vast length of the man to his smiling face. When his masculine beauty struck her full force, her mouth sagged open.

"You're much better looking in person, too," he said with a gentle, arrogant smile. Then he moved away—toward Kate's door.

As he pushed it open, he heard Esther buzzing Kate frantically. "I'm sorry, Kate. I—I couldn't stop him! Keith Jones is on his way in."

"Call security," Kate ordered brusquely just as Jim

Keith walked up to her desk, seized the phone, and replaced it in its cradle.

"Why, it's…it's you," she gasped, her horrified eyes trailing up the long length of him just as Esther's had. Kate turned purple. "You're…that awful yard-man."

He forced a smile. "Not awful—surely. Think of me as your gallant rescuer."

"You should have told me who you were Saturday!"

"It was more fun not to."

"I don't like being made a fool of. You'll pay for that little joke, Mr. Jones. Do you hear me?"

"With what? You're already set to take over everything I own," he countered pleasantly.

"A snake with your vile sense of humor deserves to go under."

"Just like a rich witch like yourself deserves to trample everyone in her path. You've taken a lot of other men's properties. Did they all deserve to go under, too?"

"Oooooo!"

"Baby, I learned a long time ago there's no justice in this world."

He leaned over and grabbed the file she had on him and his properties. When she got up, he waved her down and snapped the manila folder open and thumbed through it, quickly scanning the bleak numbers.

He whistled. "You damn sure have the goods on me!"

"I know everything about you, Mr. Jones."

"Everything about my financial predicament," he clarified. Looking up, his dark face was weary with defeat. "But not everything. Still, you're thorough," he admitted grimly.

For some reason she didn't feel like gloating. Her mouth felt too tight to smile. "I try to be businesslike, Mr. Jones."

"Ruthless! You certainly have me by the—"

"Which is right where I want you."

"Indeed?" His brazen gaze swept below his belt and then back to her with a derisive grin.

Her swift blush of humiliation was not nearly so satisfying as he'd anticipated. Instead he was moved by her wide vulnerable eyes. She was scared. Fortunately, before he said anything mushy or stupidly comforting, two burly security guards rushed in.

"Take him," Kate ordered coldly, recovering herself.

"I could have turned you over to the cops Saturday," Jim Keith whispered as the men moved toward him. "I knew who you were. Or I could have let you drown at the bottom of my pool. Instead I saved your life."

She didn't answer. She refused to look at him.

Her men grabbed his shoulders. "Let's go, mister."

Jim Keith shrugged them away. "Kate, for God's sake, you've won," he whispered. "I just came over here because I'd really like to talk to you."

She continued to stare down at her desk. She clenched her hands, and he saw that her knuckles were white. He was almost surprised when she uttered a strangled whisper to her two men. "You can go for now. I'll buzz you—if I need you."

When they were alone again, she got up and went to the window and, turning her back, stared down at the city. The sunlight backlighted the sexy shape of her body, and he remembered just how good she'd looked naked in his bed. His loins tightened.

Suddenly her vast office seemed airless. His suit felt like a straitjacket, and he was tugging at his tie.

"So—what could we possibly have to talk about?" she asked in a quiet, businesslike tone.

"I need more time," he rasped. "Six months."

"I am afraid not."

"You were born rich," he began.

She breathed deeply. Which made her breasts rise and fall. Which made him feel hotter. He yanked the knot of his tie loose.

"A harder fate than you can possibly imagine," she whispered. "My mother died, and my father... I ran away when I was five and lived with an older, childless aunt for a year. Then my father took me away from her and put me in boarding schools. I hardly saw him—until I was grown."

"The finest schools, I'm sure. And after that you languished at Harvard and Cornell."

Languished... "Yes...." She nodded.

Jim Keith tried not to see the tears in her eyes. He forced a hard note into his voice. "Well, I was born poor, which might be a tougher fate than you could imagine, honey. I would have given anything to have the time or the money to get even one college degree—here locally. You have three eastern degrees."

"Lucky me." She caught herself. "Look—I thought you wanted to talk business. I've got more to do than listen to your poor-boy jealousies."

He got up slowly. "I'm not jealous of you, damn it. I wouldn't be you for anything in the world. Is your work only money, numbers…"

"What else should it be?"

"I spent years building up everything you're going to take Friday."

"I know."

He moved nearer. "But do you know how that feels? I know my stuff doesn't equal a fraction of your net worth, but I put myself into buying it. Into running it. I don't sit around in some fancy skyscraper with dozens of employees and handmaidens bringing me coffee. I know every tenant and every man who works for me. Every manager. I've overseen every repair. I've done a lot of them myself."

"Then you've spread yourself too thin. Mr. Jones, you borrowed a great deal of money three and a half years ago, and yet your properties are terribly neglected. What did you do, party it all away?"

"Party it away?" he asked, thunderstruck. He thought of Mary—sick and thin, dying even, and the money he'd borrowed to save her. Maybe he'd been a fool not to listen to the American doctors who'd warned him the German doctors would fail, but this witch's contempt made something explode inside him.

"You're in way over your head, too, honey," he growled. "What I did with the money is none of your business."

"If I could see where you'd spent a dime on your property—"

"You push. You want more, more, but nothing you get will ever be enough without—"

Later he would never know what drove him to do what he did. Later he would hate himself. But he didn't think. The rage inside him had been building for months, for years, from that first terrible moment when Mary had been diagnosed, and suddenly Kate was here—sexy Kate, his destroyer.

Kate, cruelly beautiful, magnificently beautiful with her healthily flushed cheeks and flaming hair; Kate, more wondrously beautiful and far more desirable even than his gentle Mary. Kate, who made his blood pulse with angry blazing needs he would have given anything to deny if only he hadn't been too furious and too aroused to think straight.

She looked so cool and imperious—untouched by the real world and real feelings, so untouched by the kind of unfair fate he had endured. Had she ever known the bitter taste of failure? He could not go down without making her suffer just a little, too.

So he grabbed her, his fingers sinking into her soft flesh with a crushing grip as he caught her to his hard body. Then his angry lips were devouring hers with more hunger than he'd ever felt. His tongue filled her mouth, tasting her, exploring her. Claiming her. His hands slid down her back and buttocks, arching her into his body.

And she felt good, so good that his hunger was suddenly stronger than his anger. Maybe she was hard and ruthless when it came to business, but in his arms, she became the softest and most pliant creature. She made not the slightest effort to resist him.

At first she went rigidly still, but when his mouth touched hers, she made a soft, endearing little moan that tugged at his heart. She opened her lips to his tongue. Her need seemed delicious and sweet. She seemed somehow so untouched and innocent. And suddenly he craved more of her.

Her trembling hands came around his neck, her fingers gently clutching at first and then raking through his inky hair as if she could no more deny her own feelings for him than he.

"I'm supposed to hate you," she whispered raggedly even as she clung, breathing hard, pressing her slim, trembling body into his.

"Likewise," he muttered as he lowered his mouth to hers again. This time her tongue came inside his lips, and her response aroused him to do more, to want more, until he felt himself swept near some fatal edge on a burning tide of desire.

She was his enemy, and surely God had the cruelest, the most warped sense of humor to make Kate Karlington the one woman whose look and touch could make him want to get past his grief over Mary.

But he did. He wanted to strip her and devour her slim pale body. All day Sunday, visions of her naked loveliness had haunted him.

He wanted to plunge deep inside her and stay encased in her warm velvet flesh, joined—until he made her know that she could never belong to anyone but him.

He cursed God that she who thought him a fool for

his failures was the one woman he wanted. Suddenly he knew how ridiculous she must find him. How she must despise him. This realization made her sweet-tasting, eager mouth and warm voluptuous body a torture.

He forced himself to let her go, and the instant he did, she slapped him.

Then she gasped at the livid white mark on his tanned cheek and stumbled backward. The intense emotion in her eyes was more desperately sad than angry. "Get out," she whispered. "Get out."

Her half-open, cotton blouse hung limp and wrinkled. Her lovely face was tear-streaked and swollen from his kisses. Her eyes were ravaged and pain-filled. Her hair had come out of its clip and fell in wild tangles about her shoulders.

She looked young and vulnerable, more fragile than he could ever have imagined Kate Karlington being. But more than anything, she was desirable.

"I'm sorry," he whispered hoarsely. "I shouldn't have kissed you. I just wanted to make you know that I was more than just a bunch of debits and credits in one of your files. More than a failure. I'm a man. A human being. I guess I won't blame you for cutting me to ribbons now."

He expected her to lash back at him. Instead her face softened. Her vulnerable green eyes widened, and he felt uncomfortably aware of some powerful unwanted bond with her. Her hands shook as she tried to rebutton her blouse.

Maybe she wasn't an ice-cold witch after all. Maybe the fiery softness he'd sensed in her when she'd yielded to his kisses was real. Maybe she was as lonely and as deeply hurt by life as he.

"You're wrong about me," she said, pulling her hair back nervously into her clip. "And...I'm sorry I slapped you." She reached up to stroke his rough cheek where she'd hurt him.

Her fingers were unbearably cool and light against his burning skin.

His hand closed over her delicate wrist. When he felt her pulse racing beneath his thumb, his own heart began to pound. He wanted to take her in his arms, to kiss her again.

Was he crazy?

"Mr. Jones, I don't really want to take over your properties right now. I—I would have let you have the time, but the fact is, time won't help you."

Every nerve in his hard body tightened warily.

"You need capital, Mr. Jones, and you don't have it. I do." Her voice was sweet; she almost sounded as if she really cared.

He *was* crazy. *She was his enemy.*

He cast her slim hand aside and stepped back, rejecting the comfort of her touch and her voice because he wanted them too much. "Right. You're all heart," he ground out.

"Then I'll see you Friday," she whispered as he rushed past her toward the door. "Then we'll be done with each other once and for all."

"Till that happy day," he muttered bitterly, ignoring the shimmering pain in her eyes as he stalked out.

Chapter Five

Jim Keith signed away everything he owned with an angry flourish of scrawling black ink. Then he threw his pen down in disgust and rose from the desk to his full height.

Although he didn't look at Kate, he was too aware of her sleek, long-limbed body in that exquisitely tailored, navy linen suit, and the cool perfection of her professional presence somehow magnified his masculine feelings of failure. He had spent the past week alternately hating her and hungering for her and then despising himself for the insane war going on inside him.

He glanced toward her and was struck again by how pale and exhausted she appeared this morning, as if she, too, was suffering. There were dark circles beneath her lovely eyes. She looked thinner—hardly a worthy foe. The stark truth was he'd been bested by a spoiled woman who was so fragile, he could easily have torn her apart with his bare hands. Not that he had ever physically hurt a woman, not that he even wanted to hurt her—not in that way. No, what he wanted—

Just for a second his gaze slid from her white face to the prim starched collar of her creamy blouse, which she had buttoned all the way to the top as if to conceal as much flesh as possible. He remembered another blouse, a white cotton blouse—torn open nearly to her waist, the thick cotton wrinkled from his rough lovemaking. He remembered how wantonly beautiful she'd looked, flushed from his kisses—not so perfect but somehow so human—and he wanted to be alone with her. To loosen those buttons, to touch the skin beneath the creamy cotton, to show her that although she had taken everything he owned, he could conquer her just as easily.

He squared his broad shoulders in a gesture of denial. What he had to do was get away from her, to forget her. To start over.

He grabbed his bulging briefcase and was almost out the door when she called out to him, the honey of her phonily sweet voice making his stomach claw.

"Mr. Jones, before you go, I'd like to talk to you—alone."

Although gently spoken, it was a command.

His mouth tightened as he fought against the violence he felt. Somehow he managed an indifferent shrug. "What could you and I possibly have to talk about now?"

"I have a proposition that might interest you."

Her tone was softer, beguilingly softer—it tore him apart.

Jim Keith's black gaze swept from her blazing green eyes downward, noting her curves hungrily, and thinking that despite her pallor and her prim suit, despite her extreme nervousness, she had never looked more beautiful.

"Sorry, not interested," he muttered brutally, shoving the door open with his thick briefcase.

She went white, those huge eyes of hers flickering with pain at his insulting tone. He realized suddenly that she wasn't gloating, that she hadn't really wanted to hurt him—that this foreclosure was strictly business as far as she was concerned.

Too bad he couldn't write it off as just another business deal gone sour.

The craziest thing of all was that *he* actually felt an odd pang of remorse at having hurt her.

"I really would like to talk to you," she said, her voice tighter, but nicer than he deserved.

Nicer than he wanted.

"All right. But make it fast." He yanked the heavy chair away from the desk and sat down again while the others paraded dutifully out of the room.

"Does everyone always do what you want them to?" he spat contemptuously.

She paled at some unhappy memory, but she ignored Jim Keith's thrust. "Last week, you asked me what I intended to do about the people who worked for you. About you. And I said—"

"I remember what you said. Every damned word. You don't have to repeat it. I know you're as eager to be rid of me as I am to be rid of you. I won't hold you to what you said."

"I really would like to offer you a job."

"No way."

"You haven't even heard what I have in mind."

"Look, you've now got everything I ever owned. Isn't that enough? Are you determined to gobble me alive, too?"

"No—"

"Yes. You are. Look, I've been on my own since I was sixteen. Paper route. All sorts of things. I haven't worked for anyone in years. And never for a woman. Much less for the one woman who repossessed everything I once owned. I wouldn't know how to be one of your obedient lackeys."

"I wouldn't expect you to be," she said in that thick, velvety voice.

"How could I work for you—managing properties that were once mine?"

"Lots of people have done it."

"Not me. Besides, why would you want to hire a failure?"

"I don't see you that way."

Although her kind words warmed him, he laughed mirthlessly, more determined than ever that what he really wanted was to rid himself of her forever.

"Except for that one loan three and a half years ago, your management has been superb. I have taken on a lot of properties besides yours, and I'm over-extended. I—I don't mean financially.... I really do need some managerial help." She wrote down a figure on a piece of paper and handed it to him. "This is the annual salary I'm prepared to offer you. I wish I could pay you more, but as you know, the real-estate market is precarious. I wouldn't want to make a promise I couldn't afford to keep."

He glared at the huge number and then at her, even more furious than before—because he needed the money so desperately, and she was being so generous.

No! She wasn't generous! When she wanted something, she bought it.

But the offer tempted him. So did the woman.

"Is there anything you've ever wanted and never been able to buy?" he demanded in a hard whisper.

"You might be surprised."

Working for himself, he'd never taken home nearly as much as she was offering him—which she knew. He'd plowed most of his profit back into the properties. "What makes you think I'd be worth that amount?"

"I'm sure you'll earn every penny."

He wondered what she wanted him to do to earn so much money. He sucked in a deep breath and decided it would be stupid to insult her by asking.

If he went to work for her, he'd be selling out.

If he didn't, he'd be a fool. He was dead broke. Hell, he needed the job. He would make enough so he could save, so he could eventually reinvest and begin again on his own. It wasn't as if she'd own him forever.

"I know you don't like me very much," she said softly, "but we won't have to see that much of each other."

"Is that a promise?"

"Yes." The pain in her voice tugged at some tender emotion in him he didn't want to acknowledge. "I'm sorry. About today. I—I really don't want you to hate me."

He wished he did hate her, but he remembered how cute he'd thought she was when she'd gamely taken him on about Bobby Lee's lurid reading material. He remembered her diving into that pool to save his kid. He remembered the wild terror he'd felt when he'd pulled her limp body from the pool, when he'd struggled to force air into her lungs. He remembered as well his thrill of joy when she'd spit out water and gasped that first tortured breath. Most of all he remembered how awed he'd been by the perfection of her naked body, how hungry he'd been for the taste of her mouth, how hungry he still was—and for so much more than kisses. Even though he wanted to hate her, he was powerfully drawn by her.

He wanted to work for her...and not just for the salary, and not just to find some way to exact revenge. He wanted to figure her out.

"How could I possibly like you?" he asked cruelly in response to her earlier statement. "You're a Karlington. You've bought me—like you've bought everything else you ever wanted."

"Must you always be so rude...and—and so insolent to me?"

"Why not? You have it coming. Besides, when you get to know me better, you'll find out I have a lot more flaws."

"When I get to know—"

"Yes. You see, I've decided I have no choice but to take the job. And whatever it is, I'll do my best to satisfy you, honey. At the price you've named, I am yours." As her shimmering green gaze fearfully met his, he could feel his own heart surging very hard and very fast. "And I promise you, Kate—you'll get a helluva lot more than your money's worth."

Kate Karlington had frequently remembered his promise in the three months that had followed, for never had any employee worked harder and made himself more invaluable to her than Keith, as she called him now. It was as if he was determined to prove his worth both to himself and to her.

Not that she saw much of him. He deliberately kept out of her way. And the fact that he did, only made her perversely crave to be near him. She sought him out on a thousand pretexts, and it hurt her that although he was unfailingly courteous, he remained tightly guarded around her, while with everyone else, he was genial and easygoing. With Esther he was almost flirtatious, and Kate could always tell when he was in her outer office by Esther's warm laughter. Occasionally he took Esther to lunch. And because he did, a tight, jealous coolness had come into her own relationship with her secretary.

Keith welcomed input from both tenants and managers and, to Kate's surprise, from her. He was not threatened by other people's good ideas. On those rare occasions when she chose to override him, he usually gave in gracefully. She'd known he'd be good, but not nearly as invaluable as he was. While she was steady, he was more innovative and more willing to take risks. Although they didn't think alike, their talents balanced each other. They worked well together.

He was very protective of her and wouldn't allow her to go out to troubleshoot at the tougher projects, especially at night. He handled all the difficult clients and hostile tenants himself. Thus, she was working shorter hours while her properties were better run, better maintained, safer and more profitable than they'd ever been before. There was only one thing he could be awful about: he'd repeatedly and quite arrogantly refused to help her buy discounted notes or negotiate repossessions.

Once when she'd needed to go out of town and had asked for his help with a foreclosure, she'd lost her patience and pressed him too hard.

"No," he had thundered, his control breaking. "You may think you own me body and soul, but you don't, Kate. Not quite. I won't steal for you—no matter how much I need the damned money you pay me."

"You leave me no choice—"

"Why don't you fire me, then?" he asked, his eyes blazing as he strode toward her. He was so furious, he had forgotten what she suspected was his unwritten code—to keep to the opposite side of any room he was forced to share with her.

Kate glanced fearfully up at him. Physically he was so huge and powerfully built, he could have done anything to her.

Not that he raised either of his large, tightly clenched, brown fists. Still, she backed away just a little, licking her dry mouth.

"Why don't you put us both out of our misery? Fire me. Then we'll finally be rid of each other." His eyes met hers and then ran down her body burningly.

"D-don't look at me like that."

"Like what, honey?"

"Like you want to eat me alive."

His face tensed; so did his whole body, as he sought to curb his fierce emotion. "Maybe that's not so easy sometimes. Especially when I think you really want me to.''

"I don't!" she denied swiftly.

"You're lying. We both know it."

"No—"

He laughed. "If you don't like it, go on then, fire me. Do it, honey, and I'm outta here."

She knew he would go; she'd never see him again. Some part of her wanted that as much as he did. And yet some other part only felt alive knowing he was near.

Kate glared at him. "I—I can't."

"Then do your own dirty work," he snarled softly. "But, honey, I'm available to you—personally—anytime after hours."

"What?"

"You bought me, remember? You can have my body. Just not my soul."

His insolent macho remark cracked like a bullet. Surely he didn't think her so, low, so desperate—

"Dear God," she whispered.

His feverish gaze made her all too aware that he had meant every chilling word. He smiled wolfishly as a telltale tide of hot color crept into her cheeks.

"You are awful," she gasped. "Simply awful."

He just smiled.

She was silent.

"If you change your mind, honey, you'll have to chase me. Because I damn sure don't intend to throw myself at you again and beg you for it," he taunted.

"You're crazy if you think I'd ever, ever do that!"

His black eyes cut her like impaling shards of

razor-sharp glass. "Maybe..." His dazzling smile was equally ruthless. "But I think not."

"You coldhearted, conceited bast—"

She uttered a wild, strangled cry, but when he reached for her, she was too agitated to note that his hard face had softened with remorse and concern for her. Not wanting his pity, she pushed him away, and he stiffened as she ran blindly past him.

She had rushed home to pack and then canceled her business trip because she was too overwrought to go, and the next morning she had convinced herself that she really would have to fire him. But the first thing she saw when she walked into her office was a single red rose and a crisp white note covered in his bold black scrawl. *Forgive me. I was very angry and very rude. And I'm sorry.* That was all. There was no signature. But she sank down in her chair, clutching his note and the rose to her heart.

After that terrible confrontation, Keith was more careful than ever to avoid her. But when Keith's sister, Maggie, who often baby-sat Bobby Lee, brought the little boy to see his father at the office, Bobby Lee always left his aunt and father and rushed in to say hi to Kate. The boy seemed to sense the natural affinity she felt for children, and the two of them grew closer. The child was so open and friendly with Kate that she could easily bestow on him all the warmth and affection that his father would have coldly rejected. Maggie and she had become friends, too.

Once when Kate had been embracing Bobby Lee in a proud, motherly hug after he showed her a blue ribbon he'd won in a swim meet, she'd looked up to

see Keith standing silently in the door. His expression
had been dark, almost…almost jealous. No. She was
wrong. The last thing Keith wanted was kindness or
warmth for himself from her. He probably just resented his son developing a close attachment to her.

Something Maggie had said about Bobby Lee's
mother had made Kate increasingly curious about
Keith and about that ill-advised loan that had caused
him to lose his holdings. Since Keith always cut her
off every time she got near any subject that was re-
motely personal, Kate did what she'd always done—
she bought the information she wanted by hiring a
private investigator. And after she found out that he'd
come from a big, poor but loving family, that he'd
married his high school sweetheart whom he'd apparently loved so deeply, he'd mortgaged himself to
the hilt to try to save her when she'd become ill, Kate
had burst into tears, regretting that she'd foreclosed
on his properties.

Kate remembered how he'd come to her and
begged her to extend his loans for six months. If she'd
only known why he'd borrowed the money, she might
not have been so tough, and now he might not be so
determined to keep their relationship so cool and professional. She longed for a way to make amends, to
establish some middle ground that would lead to a
warmer, friendlier relationship, but he was so fiercely
proud and so determined to avoid her, she was baffled
as to how to approach him. When Esther, who had
become his friend, told her he'd begun to date again,
Kate felt more desolate than ever.

She was losing him.

She had never had him. So, he was the father of the most darling little boy, a child she could have easily adopted for her own.

So, Keith had stripped her and teased her. So, he had kissed her once and made her feel more wantonly alive than she'd ever known she could feel. So, he was fabulous at running her business. So, he was the most handsome hunk she'd ever known and was right about her wanting him—desperately.

To him she was merely the woman who'd foreclosed on him, and his boss, a woman he would brutally humiliate the first chance he got. She knew that he was saving his money, planning for the day when he could quit her.

Why did she care anyway? Hadn't she learned anything from Edwin? The wrong kind of relationship with Keith could prove far more devastating.

But Kate couldn't quit wanting him. One summer evening she was leaving her office late when she saw a ribbon of light beneath Keith's door. She was surprised since he usually stayed away from his office—to avoid her, she suspected. Then she remembered Esther gaily having told her he'd been forced to make a late appointment with Mr. Stewart, a difficult owner from out of town for whom they managed two thousand rental units and three strip shopping centers, all of which needed an infusion of cash.

She should have gone home; instead she knocked hesitantly on Keith's door.

He opened it himself, and as always, just the nearness of his darkly handsome face and his broad-shouldered frame in that crisp white shirt made her blood pressure rise.

"Kate," he drawled coolly, frowning, his black gaze meeting hers and darkening briefly before he forced a wary smile.

She hardly noticed Mr. Stewart's short, rotund figure rising clumsily from his chair. She was shivering from the feel of Keith's fingers at her slim back, guiding her inside, as if their relationship was an easy, harmonious one.

"I'm sorry to interrupt," she began.

"On the contrary, I'm glad you did," Mr. Stewart said.

Keith led her to the chair beside his own. "Since you're here, maybe you can convince Mr. Stewart he's going to continue to lose money if he doesn't put some real money into his properties."

Then she and Keith worked together, as though they were equal partners, smoothly presenting their arguments, backing each other up, and an hour and a half later Mr. Stewart handed Keith a large check and promised more.

Then Mr. Stewart was gone, and Kate was alone with Keith for the first time since that last terrible encounter.

"You were good," he said quietly, his dark eyes fastened on her face in that intense way that made her pulse race.

"So were you," she whispered, unused to praise from him and feeling too hot suddenly.

She wished she could forget that awful taunt of his, but it haunted her. *If you change your mind, honey,*

*you'll have to chase me. Because I damn sure don't
intend to throw myself at you again and beg you for
it.*

Unaware of her thoughts, he stood up and pulled
his suit jacket off the back of his chair. She got up,
too, and went nervously to the window.

If you change your mind...

Behind her he snapped the chain on his desk lamp,
and the tiny room melted into soft darkness. She became aware of the sparkling stars and the spread of
city lights and of the brilliant silver moon. It was
Friday night, a night lovers spent together. As usual,
she was set to spend it alone.

Her stomach growled unromantically.

He laughed huskily, almost easily—something he
hadn't ever done around her. "Sounds like someone
besides me worked up an appetite."

"I *am* hungry," she admitted, shyly meeting his
eyes again and feeling drawn to him as never before.
He looked away.

*If you change your mind, honey, you'll have to
chase me....*

Suddenly she realized she was starving, and not
just for food. For companionship. For Keith's companionship. For much much more than that.

He rammed his hands deep into his pockets, spoiling the fit of his suit. "We'd better get the hell out
of here."

"It's such a pretty night," she whispered, stalling,
not following him as he headed toward the door.

"Hot and humid," he said a little impatiently as
he thrust the door open.

"But pretty from here," she said, lingering still. "What do you do most Friday nights?"

"Not much," he said grimly.

"Do you have a date tonight?"

"Do you?"

"Not yet," she said.

"What's that supposed to mean?"

"I—I could buy you dinner?" *Was that chasing?*

"I don't think that's such a good idea," he countered.

Rejection. Her father had never wanted to spend time with her. She had never known how to make friends.

Why had she bothered to ask him? She felt hollow now. She should shut up and thereby salvage what was left of her wounded pride. She should leave and pretend she felt nothing. But she had no pride where he was concerned, and even to her ears, her low voice sounded too pleading.

"Look, I know you probably still resent what I did three months ago when I foreclosed—"

"Don't," he said almost sharply.

"But I'm sorry," she went on desperately in a rush. "I—I didn't know about your wife then."

"How did you find— The last thing I want to discuss with you is Mary." But his tone was softer, gentler, as if he sensed her pain.

"I—I don't blame you for hating me."

"Damn."

When she approached the door, she felt him tense as if her nearness bothered him, too, but he just stood there stiffly, waiting for her, holding the door, not looking at her.

"I know you didn't want to work for me, and still you've been wonderful—"

She walked on past him, passing so close to his body that her arm brushed his. Fleetingly she felt the warmth of him like a small electric shock.

She stopped. "Keith, you may not believe this, but I know what it feels like to lose…everything. To… fail."

"You're right. I don't believe it."

She heard his key click in the lock. She would have given anything to know what he was thinking, what he was feeling. She wondered if he had any idea how truly sorry she was.

She had always wanted love and affection and warmth, but she'd never known how to get it. Her shoulders hunched.

Then from behind her came his low voice, slower and warmer than she'd ever heard him speak to anyone. "Kate, how do you feel about barbecue?"

She whirled around, feeling a sudden overwhelming eagerness, her eyes shining. "What?"

He took her trembling hand in his and smiled. "It's yes to supper, if you'll come eat barbecue with me."

"I never do. You'll have to pick the restaurant."

"No problem. And another thing, Kate—tonight, I pay."

"You don't have to." She grinned impishly. *"I'm chasing you."*

His swift hot glance told her he knew exactly what she meant. "Are you sure?"

"Very."

For a moment he hesitated. Then his arm touched her back possessively, and he led her toward the elevator.

Chapter Six

Jim Keith was coldly furious with himself as he took a pull from his long neck and watched Kate across the crowded restaurant. She was saying hi to some tony acquaintances of hers, and from the way Kate's glamorous, blond girlfriends were eyeing him and Kate was blushing, he figured they must be teasing her about him. Since they looked like society types, they probably disapproved of her going out with a guy who wasn't part of their rich crowd. The beer was icy, which was good, because he suddenly felt so hot.

Why the hell had he let that vulnerable, pleading look of Kate's get to him and make him agree to come out with her? Why hadn't he made some excuse and said he planned to spend the evening with Bobby Lee? Why did sharing a simple dinner with Kate have to seem so dangerous?

Because she had said, "I'm chasing you," in that sweetly beguiling way that had made his flesh feel tight and wild. That made him know how much he wanted her.

Because just finding himself alone with her in the velvet darkness of his car had made him forget they came from two different worlds, made him forget that she was rich and he was a failure. More than anything, he had hungered fiercely to pull the car over and put his hands all over her.

Not that she had come on to him again during the short drive to the restaurant. She'd seemed as tense and shyly nervous as he—as if she'd regretted asking him.

He took another pull from the bottle as he remembered that drive. While he'd turned on the air-conditioning full blast, she'd flipped his radio to a booming rock station. But the jungle beat had only fired his blood. When he'd finally stopped at the restaurant, her fingers had been so shaky, she hadn't been able to unfasten her seat belt. She'd cried out in frustration, and he'd turned off the radio and helped her, saying hoarsely and yet gently, "Look, we can forget you said it. You can still back out—"

"So can you," she had whispered.

And maybe he would have if she hadn't reached across the darkness almost reluctantly and touched his rough cheek with those tender, trembling fingertips, if she hadn't then buried her face gently in the hollow of his neck for a long moment, drawing a deep, shaking breath. If he hadn't taken her in his arms and held her comfortingly. If she hadn't felt so small and warm, so utterly defenseless and yet so deliciously feminine—so damnably right.

Just when he'd figured she'd never have the guts, she'd picked up the gauntlet he'd so cruelly thrown down. If she'd capitulated earlier, she wouldn't have been half so dangerous. But now he no longer saw her as some cruel, avaricious vulture who'd mercilessly stripped him. Even if she was too rich and too elegant, too well educated and too hung up for someone of his more common background, he also saw that she was vulnerably human. He was beginning to see that her cold rejecting father had made her feel worthless and unlovable.

Keith had also grudgingly come to admire certain aspects of her character. Despite her money, she didn't behave condescendingly to him. She didn't shirk work, and she seemed to appreciate his. They both had high energy levels. She genuinely loved kids. Indeed, she was always so sweet to Hannah and Bobby Lee that at times Keith was almost jealous of his own son.

Nor could Jim Keith deny that she was the cause of his starting to get over Mary. Whenever Kate came within five feet of him, every muscle in his body got so tense and hard, it was all he could do not to seize her and show her how much he wanted her. That was why he'd been so awful to her and tried to force her to fire him when she'd pushed him about helping her with that repo. He hadn't known how he could go on working for her, wanting her and pretending he didn't.

But she hadn't fired him even when he'd hurt her. And he'd realized he would have been even more miserable if she had. So he'd played this waiting game, his pride demanding that she, who was so far above him socially and monetarily, she who was his boss, humble herself and come to him.

He didn't like her being richer and probably smarter than he was, but he had found more to like about her every day. He had always been confident about his appeal to women, but the opposite was true of her. She had no idea how attractive she was. He hadn't ever seen her flirt with another man. He felt sorry for her, and yet at the same time he was glad she lacked confidence with other men. That made the fact that she found him attractive and was brave enough to show it all the more special.

Thus, what he felt now was much more powerful than a mere physical attraction or that initial vengeful desire to get even. If she was confused, so was he. He knew she was afraid of him, afraid of all men, and yet hellishly compelled anyway. Just as he was.

He'd taken Esther to lunch to learn about Kate. Esther had described Kate's motherless childhood, her cold, rejecting father, the lonely boarding schools, and Edwin's marrying her for her money and then breaking her heart by leaving her, forcing her to deal with the unexpected pregnancy alone. But the thing that had hit him the hardest was what Esther had said about Kate's miscarriage.

"She was like a ghost when she came out of that hospital," Esther had said. "When Edwin didn't come to the memorial service, Kate wouldn't let anyone else comfort her. We were afraid that she might do something desperate, but slowly she got better."

Jim Keith's heart had gone out to Kate for her lonely life. Since he'd always had to work so hard for every dime, since she was rich and he was broke, she probably saw him as a money-grubbing bastard who could never be interested in her without ulterior motives. She'd probably think he was after her money or revenge. Then he'd played on her fears and made things worse by saying he'd sold her his body.

Damn—he regretted that.

From across the room, Kate smiled shyly at him again, and the vulnerable warmth in her eyes lit every part of him. A long shuddering wave of desire racked him as he studied the lush curve of her mouth and remembered her sweet taste. His hand froze on the long neck. Then slowly he raised the bottle to his lips and tried to quench his hot thirst for her with another icy swig.

But Kate couldn't seem to quit looking at him, and as he drained the bottle, he knew nothing but the taste of her lips could ever satisfy him. He set the empty bottle down and shoved it away, easing his long body slowly off the wooden bench.

As if in a dream, she moved toward him, too. Behind her the red-and-white-checkered tablecloths and blinking neon beer sign that hung on the wall blurred hazily.

They met halfway across that smoky, crowded room—on the edge of the dance floor, standing so close, they could have touched, and yet not touching as the silence between them grew as hot and taut as his nerves. Someone put a quarter in the jukebox, and the throbbing rhythm and the singer's melancholy crooning only magnified the tense longing he felt for her.

"Dance with me," she whispered.

His breath caught as she came into his arms. She stretched onto her tiptoes; one of her slender hands reached up and clutched his wide shoulder, and just that feather-light touch against his crisp cotton shirt brought a sudden flare of heat to every male cell in his body.

"Kate..." he said hoarsely, warningly.

Her light fingertips moved across his shoulder to his throat. "Please, Keith. Hold me."

When her warm breath whispered across his skin, he knew he was lost.

"Why the hell not?" he muttered thickly as his hard arms circled her closely.

When she pressed her slim body into his, his blood began to pound with a furious rush. He crushed her so tightly against his chest that he could feel her nipples grow erect beneath her thin silk blouse. Instinctively her slim body swayed so perfectly with his that it seemed they'd been dancing together all their lives. And yet, it wasn't that way at all. For she was thrillingly, wondrously new to him.

He lowered his dark head and saw that her inky lashes were trustingly closed against cheeks that were rapturously aglow. His hand stole slowly up and down her back, beneath the thick waves of her silky hair, molding her to him even more tightly until his every breath was hot and raspy. Until his heart thundered, until his blood coursed through his arteries like fire. Until the music and the beer and the soft perfumed essence of her voluptuous body worked together to destroy what was left of his iron control.

They were only halfway through the song when he felt too wretchedly turned on to take another step. Sweat was beading his dark brow when he broke away from her abruptly.

In the dimly lit restaurant, she looked at him with wide, unafraid eyes, her red hair curling against her pale face. And he thought never had any woman seemed more beautiful.

"What's wrong?" she asked innocently.

"Either we get the hell out of here and I take you to bed—now, or we sit down and order," was all he could manage.

She almost sprinted to their table. He followed at a slower pace. They ordered ribs and sausage and more beer.

Maybe it was the beer that got him talking. Maybe it was just Kate—looking at him with those adoring green eyes as if she hung on his every word. Whatever it was, he forgot how rich and socially wrong she was for him and broke every damned rule he'd ever made about how he'd behave around her.

He'd sworn he'd never get personal. To his horror he found himself telling her about Mary, how he'd loved her, how happy they'd always been even when they'd been poor, how he'd wanted to die when she'd died, how he'd felt so guilty about failing to save her that he hadn't cared much about real estate for a long time, how he'd gone on living only because of Bobby Lee. But how lately he'd been glad he had—because of Kate.

Most women didn't want to hear about another woman, but Kate seemed so genuinely interested in him that he couldn't stop talking. At several points, her hand had closed over his, and it was as if he gave her his pain and she willingly took it.

He told her about his habit of drinking on Mary's

birthday and on their anniversary, about how he'd been doing that the night before he'd met her and that was why he'd deliberately goaded her that first day. He told Kate that even when he'd thought he'd hated her, from the minute he'd seen her sneaking onto his property, he'd stopped grieving so much for Mary.

Not that he told Kate everything. Not that he admitted the reason he'd worked so hard for her was to please her, to win her admiration, her respect. Not that Kate confided in him. But she listened, and he felt a deeper closeness to her.

The evening would have been ordinary, had his feelings for Kate not been so dazzling that even the ordinary became wonderful. After they ate, he called Maggie and made sure she didn't mind Bobby Lee's sleeping over. Then he drove Kate down to Galveston, and they walked along the beach, talking still. Later he took her to a nightclub to dance. And all too soon he found himself inside her elegant sky-rise apartment, sipping Scotch from her expensive crystal as he held her in his arms and looked out upon her magnificent view of the sprawling city and the Galleria. Then he was kissing her, and her body was melting into his, her mouth and skin sweeter and more intoxicating than the smoothest, hottest liquor.

He had no idea how he negotiated the dark halls and circular stairway as he carried her up to her bed, nor how he got her undressed and into that bed. All he knew was that when he fitted her naked body to his, when her legs wrapped around his waist and her voluptuous lips caressed his mouth and throat, this was what he'd craved from the first moment he'd set eyes on this lush, vibrant, passionate creature.

Her careful control was gone. She was writhing and twisting; and her warm flesh stirring against his thighs set him aflame. He caught her to him and held her tightly as she impatiently urged him into that final, most intimate embrace. He kept trying to go slow, and she kept passionately urging for more. Only in that last moment, when he was ready to plunge deeply inside her, did he remember that he had to protect her.

''Just a minute, honey,'' he murmured, his heart thudding violently as he released her.

Leaning across her trembling body, he fumbled for his wallet on the floor. He had the thing out of the wrapper and was pulling it on when her velvet-soft voice stopped him.

''No,'' she whispered in that same beguiling tone that had tempted him to come out with her tonight, gently trying to push his hand away. ''You don't have to put that on.''

Her soft, warm, soothing lips moved along his neck while her seeking hands explored his body, tempting him from his purpose, and for an instant he did forget everything except the exquisite torture of those slim hands circling his manhood.

Then he was on fire to enter her. But he had always taken responsibility for any woman he'd ever made love to, and not even passion could make him set aside his fierce principles. He had to protect her from the consequences of tonight's lovemaking.

You don't have to put that on, she had said.

Why the hell not? he wondered.

Her fingertips lightly stroked his silken male flesh in delicate circular motions until he shivered, tightening, until he felt he'd burst in her hand if he didn't get inside her.

He was panting hard—dying for her. Every nerve cell in his body urged him to take her.

She opened her body so that he could slide inside her.

"Are you on the Pill?" he demanded.

He felt her tense before she reluctantly whispered, "No. But it doesn't matter, darling." She reached for him with trembling hands and tried to coax him forward into the velvety warm, satin softness he was aching for.

But he couldn't. Not till he knew why she didn't want him to protect her.

He saw her radiantly tender face when she was with his son, and stronger than Keith's passion to have her was the sudden, coldly intelligent realization that she wanted far more from him tonight than mere sex.

Very gently his hard hands wrapped hers and wrenched them from his waist. She gasped as if in pain. His own loins cramped as he bolted out of the bed and strode angrily toward her window.

"What's wrong?" she called to him.

"You tell me."

"I don't know."

"Don't lie to me, damn it. This is some sort of setup. I want to know what's going on. Why did you ask me out? Ask me here? To your bed? What do you want?"

"You."

The husky torment in that raspy sound tore his heart, but he laughed harshly, bitterly. "Are you so desperate for a husband that you'd try to manipulate me into getting you pregnant, so I'd marry you?"

Silent tears leaked from the corners of her eyes as she turned her face away. "No."

"Honey, that's a lousy way to trap a man."

"I—I never wanted to trap you. I just wouldn't mind having a—" She stopped herself as if she realized it would be stupid of her to admit anything.

And suddenly he knew, and the truth chilled him more than the thought she might want to marry him.

She wasn't after him. She had never wanted him. Why should she? On that first day she'd seen him as some immoral, oversexed, low-class stud. As some failure. Despite his work to win her respect, that's probably how she still saw him.

Hell, she'd bought him, hadn't she? How could she respect him? Especially when he'd even taunted her that he'd throw his body into the bargain if she chased him hard enough? Maybe that gibe put him partly at fault, but he was furious at her anyway. Furious and hurt because all her heated passion tonight had been a lie…to trick him, to use him.

"You just wanted a baby? So—that's what tonight was about?"

She was sobbing.

"My baby?" he demanded cruelly. "Or just any dumb stud's baby?"

"I—I didn't think it out."

"Like hell." He didn't flatter her or himself by

giving her the benefit of the doubt. "If you'd gotten pregnant, you wouldn't have even thought I deserved to know. You wouldn't have told me, would you?"

As she continued to weep soundlessly, he scooped up his slacks and shirt and stalked furiously out of her bedroom.

He would never have thought that a woman who'd been so softly willing could have made him feel so lousy and hurt and cheap—so bruised to his very soul.

Maybe he deserved this. Every intelligent instinct had warned him to stay the hell away from Kate Karlington.

And in the future he damn sure would.

Chapter Seven

The week since Keith had stormed out of her apartment had been busy and very confusing for Kate. Keith's fury, which she considered unreasonable, had persisted. He hadn't come to work for three days, and when he finally did, he worked with a cold, silent efficiency that terrified her.

Not once did he so much as look at her, nor voluntarily speak to her, or refer to that night, but she knew that the injury she had done him had made him as miserable as she was. She wanted to go to him— to apologize, to beg his forgiveness. At the same time she didn't quite know what to say or how to say it.

What had happened had made her realize how desperately she wanted him, and how much she really did want a baby—before it was too late. And somehow when he'd been making love to her, these two longings had forged themselves into one. It wasn't as if she'd deliberately seduced him to get pregnant. It was just that after they'd ended up in her bed, and he'd made her aware of that possibility, she'd hadn't wanted to do anything to prevent it.

Which had started her thinking.

Was it really so terrible that she'd wanted his baby? It wasn't as if she'd intended to hold him responsible. She had thought he would be happy to have sex with

no strings attached. What other man had ever wanted
a deep involvement with her?

Her father had never wanted a real relationship.
Nor had Edwin, who had married her only for her
money. When she had been in the hospital after mis-
carrying their child, never once had either of them
come to see her. She had felt so lonely then she had
wanted to die.

Was Keith a different breed?

Every time she looked at Keith, she remembered
how wild and dark his flushed face had been right
before he'd sprung away from her. He'd wanted her
badly, as badly as she wanted him. And even now,
when he was so cold and sullen, she knew he avoided
her because he still wanted her. So they stayed apart,
each a tightly coiled bundle of nerves, each lashing
out at everybody else until the entire office staff was
as cross and irritable as a spring forest full of grumpy
bears.

Thus, when Esther walked into Kate's office frowning late on that rainy Friday afternoon, to tell her that
a female tenant had been robbed of her rent money
and then pistol-whipped while using a pay phone outside the project to call the police, Kate had lashed out
at her secretary unfairly.

"Well, what are you telling me about it for? Isn't
this the sort of thing that gives you the excuse to go
running into Keith's office for a long private chat behind closed doors?"

"For your information, I have tried to reach him.
Not that I'm the one who's so interested in him. Only
I can't get him on his car phone. He's supposed to

be in Spring at Mr. Stewart's shopping center, but Mr. Stewart says he never showed up.''

"Then I'll go," Kate said, jumping up restlessly.

"Keith'll be furious. You know he doesn't want any of the women on that property—especially this late in the afternoon.'' It was the project where Kate had first met Keith.

"Good! I hope he does get mad! I'm sick and tired of his chauvinism.''

"Honey, you've had him mad night and day ever since last Friday.''

"Oh—so you noticed!''

"Yes, and it's time you two started snapping at each other instead of at me!''

"You're so right!''

Kate wasn't so eager for a fight by the time she reached the project. In the dark the shabby project looked more ominous than it had the day she'd met Keith. When she saw several shadowy figures lurking in the dark alley behind the apartments, smoking under the eaves, she shivered.

A spray of sparks showered to the earth as the men flicked their cigarettes to the ground when she parked her Jaguar. They moved toward her, only to stop when a tall man yelled from the back of a building and yelled. ''Yo!''

Keith stepped out of the shadows.

He had obviously beaten her here. He went over to them. When they finished talking, their lighters flashed as they lit fresh cigarettes and Keith rushed angrily through the misting rain toward her.

"What the hell are you doing here?" he demanded, yanking her out of her car.

"I heard about the robbery—"

His large possessive hand crushed down on her shoulder as he shoved her against her car. "I already took care of that. I gave the tenant two rent-free months and put her in an ambulance headed to the hospital. Which brings us back to why you're here when I told you to stay the hell away from this side of town."

"You just manage this property. I own it, or have you forgotten—"

"Never for a minute."

"And I'm the boss—your boss—or have you forgotten?"

"Maybe not for long. I don't want to work for anyone who makes stupid, self-destructive decisions."

In a quieter tone, she said, "I didn't think you'd care—now."

His fingers ground into her upper arm. "What the hell is that supposed to mean?"

"You know. After our date last Friday—"

With a longing that bordered on pain, her silent green eyes rose to his. His dark face was set in hard, unreadable lines.

"If you think I want you riding around in that flashy car in a neighborhood like this when it's getting dark and a woman was just assaulted for a lousy few hundred bucks, you're crazy."

In spite of his anger, she felt a tiny thrill at his obvious concern.

"Get back in your car," he ordered. "I'll drive you home."

"What about your car?"

"I'll come back for it later."

"I—I don't want to put you to that much trouble."

"Honey, that's all you've ever done." But his deep voice no longer sounded quite so stern. In fact, it was almost gentle.

"I'm sorry for Friday, Keith," she whispered, gathering her courage.

"Yeah. So am I, honey." Lightly his hands touched her damp cheek, and the warmth of his fingers flooded her with rich bittersweet yearning. "I wish we'd met some other way. I wish you were some ordinary girl. Or I wish I was some rich guy...rich enough to date you on equal terms. But I'm not. As you just so sweetly reminded me, you repossessed everything I owned, and you're my boss now. And that's that." He opened her door. "Get in the car, Kate, before you get soaked."

"So, it's over," she whispered.

"You know as well as I do it wouldn't work. You're too damned rich, and I'm too damned proud."

She nodded reluctantly.

The windshield wipers slashed back and forth. He drove fast, even though it was pouring and the freeway was under construction—he drove as if he was very angry and wanted to be rid of her as soon as possible.

"But I—I can't forget what a wonderful time I had with you that night," she murmured.

"You will," he said grimly. "We have to, but it

was good, too good. You know, Kate, Esther told me about Edwin and...the baby you lost. I'm sorry...."

"I—I didn't realize how much I still want a child...."

"I figured that one out, too, honey." Again his voice was curiously gentle.

"I was so happy when I was pregnant. It was like I already knew the baby and loved it. Maybe all new mothers feel that way, or maybe it was just that I've never had anybody all my own."

"Find a rich guy the next time. Have his damned baby."

"I didn't mean to use you. I—I didn't even think about getting pregnant till you stopped to get that thing—"

"Okay. Maybe I can buy that."

"But I thought you'd be getting something out of, er, the encounter, too."

"You don't just go to bed with some jerk and have his kid because you want a kid that day," he said tightly as he drove up the ramp into her parking garage and eased her car into its numbered space and cut the headlights.

"You're not some jerk, and I do want a child. Is that so wrong, Keith?"

"Yes! Think of the kid. You should get married first. Kids need fathers, too."

Not the kind of father she had had.

But as she looked at Keith, she felt an involuntary twist of tender longing. He cared a great deal about Bobby Lee. She had always known that not all fathers were like hers. She remembered how jealous she'd felt of school acquaintances who spoke adoringly of their fathers.

It was utterly dark, so all she could see of Keith was the shadowy outline of his carved profile. Maybe if she had been able to see him better, she would never have been so bold.

"*I should get married....* Is that a proposal?" she whispered.

"Hell, no."

"Then you're going to make me humble myself and beg you for it—again?"

"What?"

"I'm asking you to marry me, you big, beautiful, hunky, poor-boy Neanderthal," she said, shocked and embarrassed by her own forwardness even as she touched his cheek. Even as her mouth fused hotly with his.

A wave of shockingly intense desire pulsed through them both as he curved his hand around her neck and slanted her tantalizing lips against his.

From deep in his throat he groaned, "Oh, God.... Kate, what are you doing to me?"

"I assure you my intentions are most honorable this go-round."

Her proposal of marriage tempted him even more than her generous salary had tempted him three months ago when she'd asked him to go to work for her.

"No!" Keith thundered ten minutes later when they were alone in her luxurious apartment and he'd downed his second Scotch. "No way! Kate, are you crazy? You don't love me. I don't love you. The last thing you want is to be stuck with me for life when all you really want is a baby.''

"You were the one who informed me that babies need fathers and so honorably suggested marriage," she said primly, defending herself. "Not me. I was perfectly willing to forgo that sacred institution and just try to get pregnant on my own.''

"That wouldn't be fair to the…to *our* baby.''

"Okay. So, I'll concede that point—I believe you did tell me once that your morals were more old-fashioned than mine," she agreed sweetly, pouring him a third glass of Scotch. "I didn't believe you at the time. But I'm beginning to see that you're not the man I thought you were at all.''

"If you're trying to get me drunk, I can hold my liquor," he growled, not trusting her. Not trusting himself.

"I know.''

"How would it be fair to me or you if we married each other when neither of us really want marriage?''

"What if marriage gave us something we did want? And what if it was only for a year?''

"What?''

"Maybe less than that. And why wouldn't it be fair—if we both got something we wanted? I know you're attracted to me, and I… Well, you know I feel the same way about—''

He felt a hot shiver of unwanted excitement go through him.

"You little fool, that's not enough to base a marriage on.''

"Okay, but it would be a big perk...at least for me."

In spite of himself he smiled.

"And suppose I agreed to tear up the foreclosure papers on your properties and extend your loans with a very generous interest rate—say over the next five years—if you married me for that year...."

"You'd go that far—"

"I want a baby...more than anything. *Your baby.* The second I'm pregnant, you can pack your bags and I'll grant you a divorce. You'll have your property back. And I will retain all rights to the child."

All rights to his child! She wanted to have his child and then to be rid of him. Suddenly the smooth Scotch scalded his throat like acid. *Nothing had changed.*

"Why, you make it sound as simple as just another...foreclosure deal." His voice was so low, at first she didn't catch the soft menace in it. Then his hand jerked, and the crystal glass he'd been holding flew wildly against the wall where it exploded into millions of sparkling, razor-edged pieces. His deep voice exploded with the same violence. "Why am I surprised you think I'm that low? When that's what you've thought since the day you met me? You think because you took my properties so easily, you can take everything else just as easily...including my self-respect."

"Keith, I—I...I didn't mean..."

"Goodbye, Kate. I'd be willing to do a lot of things to get my properties back, but I'd never sink so low as to sell my own child."

Desperate to prevent his going, she raced in front of him and threw herself in front of the door. "All right. All right. I hadn't thought of that—that you'd feel like that."

"Why the hell not? Because you see me as some subhuman?"

If she hadn't looked so utterly desperate, he would have shoved her aside and walked out for good.

"Keith…I—I think I'm beginning to see that you're really nothing like any man I've ever known. Not my father…not Edwin…. They didn't care about women or relationships or children or…"

Words could never have stopped him, but that look of forlorn agony in her beautiful eyes made him hesitate a second longer. Then he tried to push her roughly aside.

But she clung to his arm.

"Save your strength for the next man on your list of contenders to be your…your baby machine," he roared because the mere thought of other men ever touching her stabbed him with jealous anger.

"I don't have a list," she said very softly. *"There's only you."*

She felt the strong grip of his hands on her arms, pulling her against him.

"Why me?" he demanded gruffly as she nestled instinctively against the hard comfort of his warm, muscled chest and listened to the thudding rhythm of his heart. "Why me, you little fool?"

"I'm not sure. For one thing, I trust you. And I do respect you. You've earned every dollar I've ever paid you and more. You didn't sleep with me when you could have. You don't pretend you feel more than you do.''

"Maybe I just thought you were smart enough to see through me if I did.''

"Keith, all my life I've been so lonely and so terrified of loneliness," she whispered. "The other girls at my boarding school went home on the weekends, but I never could. I just want somebody of my own, somebody I can love who maybe someday will love me. I know most of the men I might marry would really be marrying me for my money, and I don't want that kind of marriage again…where I think I'm loved, and I'm not. I—I promise you I won't be the indifferent kind of parent my father was. And if you wanted the baby as much as I do, I would never take it away from you. You could see it, and love it as much as you wanted to. I would want you to. I just never imagined…''

And Keith, who understood loneliness and need, was lost.

"Kate. Oh, God, Kate.'' Maybe she'd had money, but she really hadn't ever had much else. Maybe there was something of real value that she needed from him.

The hot moistness of his breath comfortingly touched her nape. Slowly he squeezed her slim shaking body more tightly against his as his own emotions raged out of control.

She shivered as his lips moved burningly through her hair, across her cheek.

"I must be getting as crazy as you," he murmured. "The answer's yes.''

Then his mouth claimed hers in a shattering kiss that brought something far deeper and more mysteriously profound than mere physical pleasure. It seemed to her that when his mouth touched hers, his soul touched hers. But, of course, such a thought was ridiculous. She didn't love him. And he certainly didn't love her. Hadn't he said she could have his body—but never his soul?

But after the kiss was over, her eyes remained blissfully closed, her body warmly aflame, her thoughts sweetly tumbled and hazy. As he held her, she could feel the steady hammering of his heart, the disturbed huskiness of his breathing. He was every bit as aroused as she.

"Kate?"

She opened her eyes drowsily when he shook her and stared at his smoldering gaze and darkly carved features. "You're so good-looking," she said dreamily. "So—so sexy."

"I'll marry you, honey—but on my terms. Not yours."

He really was the most impossible man. She licked her lips. *But he was terribly handsome. And he did kiss divinely.* She forgot everything when he kissed her. She pursed her lips expectantly.

"First," Keith began sternly, "Bobby Lee will move back in with Maggie. I will live with you during the week, but I will visit him every Saturday and Sunday during the daytime hours and come home to you after five."

"But I don't mind him living with us. In fact I would love having him around—"

"Kate—no! He hardly remembers Mary, and he already sees you as more of a mother figure than I like. I don't want him becoming too attached when you'll be so temporary in his life."

She felt oddly hurt. Left out.

"That's not all. You will give me control of my former properties as well as your company for the year we're married. And we stay married, not till you get pregnant but until the baby's three months old. And if you do get pregnant, when you're three or four months along, you'll stay home and take care of yourself while I work...."

"That's impossibly chauvinistic...."

"If you're determined on this crazy plan, I won't have the mother of my child or my child at risk, while you drive yourself at the office. I know how hard you work. I know what happened to you the first time, how terribly hurt you were. Honey, you would never have come up with this crazy scheme if you were over that miscarriage."

That much was true.

"And," he continued, "when we do divorce, I'll pay child support, and I'll want generous visitation rights."

"Is that all?"

He nodded.

Strangely enough she wasn't nearly as furious at his preposterous terms as another woman might have been. She remembered how tired she'd gotten in the fourth month, how indifferent Edwin had been about her health. She heard herself agree weakly, wantonly.

"Oh, all right." She sighed. "But only if you kiss me again."

"I think kissing has landed us both into enough trouble for one day."

"But we're formally engaged now," she protested, her heart pounding.

Apparently he wanted her lips as much as she wanted his. And when that devastating kiss had turned into a dozen expertly placed all over her body and she found herself sprawled half-undressed beneath him on her couch, again he refused to let her seduce him.

"Stay the night," she begged, loosening his tie.

"No, Kate."

She pulled his tie through his collar and let it fall to the floor. "Why not? We're getting married."

He got up and moved to another chair. "Because if you got pregnant first, you might welsh on me. Then I'd lose you, my property and all rights to my kid."

"You're tough."

"So are you, honey. This is probably not much more to you than just another foreclosure deal. But I'm risking everything I care about."

After he left, she felt lonely and dissatisfied. But for some reason as she crawled into bed, aching for the feel of his arms around her, his parting words brought more comfort than pain. Every time she remembered the way his eyes had seared her, a tremor went through her. Because in that last moment he had made her feel that she meant everything to him.

Chapter Eight

"Well, it's about time you showed up," Kate said softly, fighting to conceal her ripple of excitement as she closed her desk drawer quickly. She didn't want Keith to see her mirror and comb and lipstick tube and realize she'd been anxiously primping because of him.

Keith's avid black gaze burned across her face and then down her body, but he said nothing.

"I left word with your secretary hours ago that all of the prenuptial documents were ready. I thought maybe you were going to change your mind and...jilt me," she said quietly.

"No way," he whispered but with such force that he startled her.

For an instant his eyes locked on hers again with that unnerving intensity. She wondered what he was thinking, what he was feeling when he moved toward her.

"Here are the papers...." she began, leaning down to pick them up.

"They'll wait," he murmured tightly, tossing them back down on her desk. They scattered messily, several white pages falling to the floor.

Before she could stoop to retrieve them, he gathered her hands and pulled her to him, holding her so close, she felt the dizzying heat of him deep inside her body. "You look especially beautiful today. So beautiful, it's hard to concentrate on the business aspects of our marriage."

She had dressed carefully to make him think that, and yet the passion in his voice was so much more than she had expected, and she was filled with a strange longing that made her feel awkward and unsure.

"Keith, you don't have to woo me," she said in a strangled tone.

"Maybe I want to," he muttered harshly.

A shadow of pain crossed her face and she turned away from him. "But you don't have to. You know this is a done deal."

"I bought you something," he said, his voice tighter and harder as he slipped a tiny velvet box into her fingers before he let her go.

She opened the box and could not quite suppress a gasp of pleasure when she saw the small but very lovely diamond winking at her from the black satin interior.

Humbly she touched the stone and then jerked her hand back. She was stunned by the thoughtful, romantic gesture. And happy. So happy, she was afraid.

"Do you like it?" he asked in a low, guarded tone, taking the ring out and slipping it on her finger. "I know it's not very big."

His ring on her finger felt far more binding than the fat stack of documents her lawyers had compiled. And far more wonderful.

"You...you shouldn't have. I mean you can't possibly afford it," she whispered, striving for control.

"You didn't have to..." Then she blurted, "You know this isn't a real marriage."

His hand tensed on her wrist and he yanked her nearer. "I know, damn it. But maybe I could forget it—if you didn't constantly remind me."

Did he want to forget it? As much as she did?

Before she could ask or argue further, his hard mouth was on hers, kissing her angrily at first and then with surprising gentleness. When his warm lips played across hers and opened them, a moan of unadulterated pleasure escaped her.

He pulled back but continued to hold her so that her face was nestled against his throat.

"Kate, are you going to throw my poverty up to me for the rest of my life? Do you ever think of us as two human beings? As just a man and a woman?"

She turned pale and began to tremble. How could she ever explain that she was far too terrified of dreams of such happiness to ever hope they could feel that way about each other?

"I'm sorry," he muttered when she didn't answer. His dark face was grave. "I shouldn't have asked. I shouldn't push you. Like you said, this is a done deal. You spelled out the rules, and I agreed to them. You don't want me. Just a kid. Let's leave it at that."

He let her go and, ducking his dark head, charged through the door and slammed it.

After he was gone, she stared miserably down at her slim hand, turning his ring so that it flashed and hating herself for making him unhappy. She had stupidly spoiled a moment he had tried to make special.

She halfway expected him to back out of their

''done deal.'' But five minutes later his secretary was at the door with a terse note from Keith demanding the legal documents.

Within minutes he had signed them, and they were back on Kate's desk.

As she stared at his bold black signature, she remembered the day he'd coldly signed over his properties to her. Suddenly she was more frightened than ever.

Not that he gave her time to be afraid for long. Keith rushed her to plan the wedding quickly.

So they could get it over with, he said brutally when she asked why he was in such a hurry.

And one week later they were married.

Still, in that limited time, Kate had made sure that her second wedding was far grander than her first. She made all the lavish arrangements to prove to her wealthy family that she was proud of her new husband and future marriage, never realizing that her groom might find the ceremony stilted and their elegant reception at the city's poshest country club pretentious and stuffy.

Keith, bored and weary from the much-rehearsed ceremony, from the long photographing session afterward and then from standing more than an hour in the receiving line, ignored several icy looks of disapproval from his new family and bride and excused himself, leaving a white-faced Kate behind while he wandered restlessly through the well-heeled throng.

His tux was rented, and his black tie felt itchy and tight around his neck. Maybe this was what a real wedding was supposed to be like, but it was beginning to feel as dreary as a funeral. Maybe that was because Kate's family didn't try to conceal that they thought he wasn't good enough for her.

He felt their eyes boring into his back as he made his way cynically to the tables piled with elegant food. He thanked the Lord for his uncle John, who was laughing too loudly from the champagne and drawing some of the stuffy Karlingtons' disapproval away from himself. Bobby Lee was taking his share of the heat, too. More Karlingtons were frowning at the boy for chasing several of his Jones cousins at the far end of the ballroom.

At one point Keith had offered to corral the children, but Kate had smiled and said she wanted Bobby Lee to be happy at their wedding.

Keith was about to pick up a fancy fried chicken leg when he caught the disdainful sound of his own name drip like acid from a cultured, feminine tongue.

He whirled. But saw no one. For a second he thought the wedding was making him paranoid.

"Her father would roll over in his grave," drawled another haughty voice from behind a trellis laced with white roses.

"How could she marry so far beneath herself? Again? This one's even poorer than the first."

There was muffled laughter.

"I—I, uh, I think this one's rather more attractive than Edwin," a third woman's voice countered timidly. "And his little boy is absolutely adorable."

The others pounced.

"Of course, *you,* Mathilde…would notice that the

scoundrel's attractive…in a vulgar, primitive sort of way! Gold diggers usually are—as *you* should have learned from your own disastrous marriages! And as for being adorable, his brat is a little savage!''

Keith downed a glass of champagne in one gulp. Then he seized a second glass and made his way to the other side of the trellis.

The stoutest of the three blue-haired biddies almost dropped her glass when she saw him. But he gallantly caught it. Managing a cynical little bow, he replaced it in her much-beringed fingers.

''Why, thank you, ever so,'' she said in a chilly tone.

''My pleasure—*ladies.*''

They blushed like girls.

Keith smiled boldly and lifted his goblet. ''To the bride.… To her good fortune. And to her future happiness…with me.'' He clicked his glass to each of theirs. ''Weren't you just saying that I, uh, was a lucky man?''

The stout one almost choked.

''Don't let me interrupt your conversation,'' he continued.

''It wasn't important,'' one of them snapped.

''Indeed,'' he purred, his steely voice softening only because Kate had come up and shyly taken his arm.

''We were saying we thought your wedding was lovely, dear,'' Mathilde said timidly.

''Be happy for me, Aunt Mathilde,'' Kate whispered, casting a radiant glance at him.

The ladies' faces froze. So did Keith's smile as he

wondered why Kate's entire family believed that the only reason he could want her was for her money.

"I feel happy, too," he murmured very tenderly, very protectively, concentrating solely on his bride. His fingers tightened against the back of her satin gown as he crushed her closer. And as his lips brushed hers, he felt the primitive thrill of male possession.

She was his. And he was glad. Neither she nor the Karlingtons would have believed the truth—that neither her money nor the return of his properties had anything to do with his marrying her. She was a beautiful, desirable woman. He wanted her for herself alone. He had wanted her so much, he would have made a bargain with the Devil to have her.

And in a way that's what he had done.

Their honeymoon hideaway was an ultramodern, two-story beach house with high sloping roofs and skylights loaned to Kate by one of her wealthy relatives. Located on Bolivar Island and, therefore, vulnerable to the violence of hurricanes from the Gulf of Mexico, the mansion stood on high concrete pilings that had been sunk deep into the soft sand.

Standing on the wooden deck, Keith stared out at the silver rollers that swept the beach. The view was no better than that from his own rougher beach house on the same island. The same surf caressed the same sand with the same constant roar. The same salty breeze rushed around both houses. The same moonlight lit the night. And yet the two houses, his so shabby and this one so elegant, seemed worlds apart.

He wondered suddenly about the woman he'd married. She had played a CD of Ravel while they'd eaten lobster; he would have been just as happy with country-western music and hamburgers. She had served him the finest, driest French wine; he was so used to Texas beer, he was still thirsty.

Was there any way a man of his simple tastes and common background could ever understand a well-educated woman who'd been to every glamorous city in the world? All he knew was that he suddenly wanted to.

More than anything.

If he had acquired this sudden taste for an elegant woman, maybe he could just as easily learn to like very dry Chablis.

Who was he kidding? Why would it even matter?

Wasn't he only a male body she had bought to satisfy this need for a child she had not been able to satisfy in any other way? Wasn't she going to ditch him the second that was accomplished?

Not if he played this hand for all it was worth.

Slowly he turned his back on the dark water and walked across the deck to go inside where Kate was waiting for him.

Tonight was their wedding night. It was high time he started finding out who she was and what she really wanted from him.

Kate was sitting up in bed scribbling enthusiastically. Her brows were drawn together, her mouth pressed into a tight line as if she was concentrating very hard. He smiled. Was she composing one of her know-it-all columns for the newspaper?

He would have liked to tell her that just because she and her snooty clan had been born rich and had had opportunities, maybe they weren't all that much smarter than he was. Maybe Kate was just lucky; maybe her money had shielded her from the hard knocks that would have taught her nobody knew as much as they thought they did.

His gaze was drawn to her dark curling lashes resting on her smooth pale cheeks like tiny fans.

He had expected fancy, impractical lingerie, but her shoulders were bare above the white sheets. In the dim golden light of the bedroom, she looked fragile and innocent, incredibly lovely and as pure and sweet as a virgin.

Even if she'd bought him, even if she thought that meant she owned him, even if he were no more than that body she had temporarily hired for stud services, it had become impossible for him to hate her.

She moved, and the sheet slipped and he saw the lush curve of her breasts. He felt a sudden raw eagerness. His heart surged with what he told himself was nothing more than the most natural and selfish male desire.

Besides, it had been a long time since he'd had a woman. Too long. If she was using him, he was using her.

He closed the door heavily, so she would look up at him. But when she did, her expression was so uncertain as she bit her lip that he wondered if she felt humiliated because she'd been the one to propose. He realized he was just as unsure of his feelings for her.

Nervously she set her tablet aside and turned the

light off when he began to undress. As he ripped his trousers off, he tried not to think of all that was wrong in their relationship. This beautiful, assertive woman would be his till three months after she gave birth to his child. He had a year.

If she couldn't learn to love him, so what? He'd learned the hard way that this was no fairy-tale world. Maybe he wasn't ready for love, either.

She turned him on. By marrying her, he would get everything back that she'd taken from him. She'd get something she wanted, too.

Even if he couldn't win her, their marriage was a mutually profitable business deal. Even if their relationship didn't work out, this was a no-lose situation.

All this seemed so simple until he got into bed and caught the scent of her expensive perfume. Until he saw the tears in her shining eyes and the sudden quenching of her smile as her lips began to tremble. Until he felt the warmth of her body clinging to the sheets. Until he took her into his arms, and her slim body slid warmly against his own, arousing something deep and eternal in him that was so much more than simple desire.

His hands raced over her hot naked skin, pausing on the almost flat curve of her abdomen.

She wanted a child.

His child.

She wanted his child more than she wanted anything else in the world. Didn't she know that his child might tie her to him?

Her hands came around his neck and sifted through his thick black hair. He touched his lips to hers ever so softly, and was surprised by the sweet emotion that filled him. Then his tenderness was followed by fiercer emotions and fiercer needs. His shaking hands tangled in her long, flowing hair as he dragged her nearer.

She moaned as he ran his mouth over her, kissing her throat, her breasts, kissing her everywhere until the tart taste of her womanly essence filled him. His pulses began to throb.

And suddenly she was writhing and moaning, and the whole thing spiraled out of control as is often the case in human relationships.

Mating and creating could form the deepest of human bonds.

Her satin-smooth skin was as sweet as warm honey.

God, he wanted her so much.

He had sworn to himself he would be able to keep his distance from her—even in bed. But the passionate melting together of their bodies carried their souls, as well, and what followed between them brought a bewildering tide of glorious new feelings and hungers. As he was caught up by the force of forbidden needs, he knew that all the boundaries in his life had suddenly been shattered forever.

He had been alone.

He was alone no more.

It was as if he were her first, and she were his. It was as if all their lives they had been looking for each other. Neither understood the wild rapture that possessed them the moment that they began to make love. But the incandescent emotion that thrilled every cell of their beings utterly overpowered them.

He took her a second time, so that he could savor the wonder of her more slowly, so he could savor the glowing emotion he felt when he was inside her. She did the same, running her hands with guiltless wonder over the muscular contours of his magnificent bronzed body, reveling in him like a wanton, kissing him everywhere as he had kissed her the first time, but again it wasn't long before that strange sensual rhythm of their bodies and minds became a vital power that drew them out of themselves and swept them away from all their previous realities and carried them to a new one that was theirs alone.

When it was over, Keith fell back into himself and was terrified. He wanted to crush her close, to beg her to forget their stupid bargain and to love him.

But she believed in buying and selling. She wanted his baby—not his love. So he got up without a word, pulled on jeans and a shirt and stormed barefooted out to the beach.

He meant only to get some space and then return to her.

But she pulled on a white robe and followed him, calling to him from the balcony, and suddenly the terrible need he felt for her was way too much. He knew he would break and confess his true feelings. If she even believed him, she would probably despise him. So, instead of returning, he started running, his feet digging desperately into the wet cool sand as he sprinted away to escape the opulent mansion and the lovely woman who called down to him.

He didn't know if he would ever be strong enough to go back. Suddenly he knew this marriage could turn out to be the biggest mistake of his life.

Chapter Nine

Keith had left her. Maybe forever.

Kate had grown up in the South, but the modern South. Not being a southern belle, she had not simpered, played hard-to-get games or denied her true needs when she had been with Keith.

No, she had chased him by asking him out first, by proposing. Nor had she hidden her eagerness for him in bed.

And now he was gone.

Where was he?

Had he really found her so hopelessly undesirable that he never wanted to see her again? Had her desperate need for him driven him away? Was he going to disappear like everyone else she had tried to love?

Not even the thought that Keith had made love to her twice and might have given her a baby softened the blow of his leaving.

She'd watched him run down that beach until he'd become a fleck and dissolved into nothingness. Then she'd crept back to bed and lain in the dark, straining to hear the sound of his return above the roar of the surf, feeling even more desolate when he didn't come back than she had the night she had lost her baby.

The sun was blazing when she finally forced herself to rise lethargically from her bed. That single glance in her bathroom mirror at her hollow-eyed, soulless white face had been so terrible she had not dared look at herself again.

Their honeymoon was to have lasted a week. No way could she return to Houston and face the humiliation of everyone knowing that Keith had left her after one night.

So she stayed at the house, somehow living through the heavy hours. In the afternoon she went out on the deck and listlessly watched the endless roll of the surf as the sinking sun turned the tips of the waves and the clouds to flame.

She wished she could be numb inside. She wished that she could stop thinking, that she could stop feeling. That she could regain some control.

But it was no use. The sun disappeared, and the waters darkened quickly as the last of the pinkness vanished in the sky. And she stayed outside shivering in the lonely darkness.

The moon came up, and she thought its silver glow on the waves looked the same as it had in Keith's hair when they'd been in bed. She remembered the way he'd touched her nipples with his callused fingers. Her skin began to burn as she remembered how his mouth had roamed her body.

No!

Her anguish was suddenly so great, she wanted to scream. To die. She had to stop torturing herself by thinking of him.

She glanced away from the sparkling water to the beach where she had last seen him. Suddenly she saw a tall figure running toward her from the beach.

It couldn't be Keith.

But her heart began to pound. Thinking herself crazy, she forced herself to look away. Then she turned back, unable to resist watching the man.

There really *was* something familiar about those broad shoulders.... About the way the moonlight glowed in his black hair.

Then the man turned from the beach and headed toward her.

And she knew.

"Oh, Keith," she moaned softly, thankfully, closing her eyes and leaning back against the house, willing herself not to act too eager. But when she felt the heavy tread of his footsteps on the stairs, her eyes flew open. Her pulse raced.

He came to an abrupt stop ten feet away from her.

Shyly she lifted her head and fought to manage a haughty, controlled Karlington look.

Across the darkness he whispered huskily, "Forgive me."

How could she do anything else?

"Why did you go?" she asked, her haughty air crumpling, her false voice shattering.

His face was as gray and lined with exhaustion as her own. His deep voice cracked in an equally betraying manner. "I...I didn't think that my leaving might hurt you."

"I—It didn't...." But her voice broke again.

"Okay." In his blazing eyes she saw the most powerful emotion. "I was so afraid you'd be gone," he said humbly, holding his arms out to her. "I wouldn't have blamed you. I behaved wretchedly. You deserved better."

How could she resist such sweetly sincere humility? From a man as proud as Keith? And since she was no southern belle, she came flying into his arms.

He crushed her to him, shuddering as if just holding her aroused powerful, uncontrollable needs. Then he shoved her up against the wall of the house, and their bodies melted together.

His thrilling salty mouth was wet and hot and seeking as it covered hers. He hadn't shaved, and the rough new growth of his beard burned her skin and lips. But she was clinging, sighing, surrendering to the volcanic tide of emotion his hard lips and hands so magically aroused.

Within seconds they were both on fire.

Very gently she wrapped her legs around his waist, and he walked, carrying her like that, inside.

He ripped her clothes off and then his and made love to her in the moonlight on the thick carpet by the fireplace. He was wilder and more primitive than the night before, and he stirred her to new heights of passion that left her quivering and spent and utterly and completely his. And when it was over he didn't get up and leave her. Instead he picked her up in his arms and carried her to bed, pulling her to him beneath the sheets so that their bodies curled together like two perfectly matching spoons. They stayed that way for the rest of the night and long into the morning. And when they finally awoke, their arms and legs warmly entangled, the first thing he did was make love to her again.

He never told her where he had gone that first night nor why, and even though it worried her, she was too afraid of spoiling their new happiness to ask. And although she masked it, another dark, unspoken fear took root and grew in her heart.

If he could leave her once like that without a word—he could do it again.

But in spite of that dark, festering fear, she fought to savor every bright moment of happiness he was willing to give her, and even living with that doubt, she was happier than she'd ever imagined she could be with anyone. She grew to love everything about him, even his faults, and even his little annoying ways—like the way he always left her bathroom trashed every time he took a shower. Like the way he always tore the plastic wrapper off the newspaper and threw it absently onto the carpet.

She didn't mind that he was always grumpy until his first cup of coffee, that after work he needed thirty minutes of solitude to decompress. It didn't bother her that he couldn't hang a towel straight or that he couldn't seem to remember how to load the dishwasher right. He threw his clothes all over the living room furniture every night when he came home. But his presence was so dear, she couldn't scold him for such habits. Not when he loved to cook. Not when he sang to her as he cooked, and quite charmingly, especially since he couldn't carry a tune.

Their life together quickly fell into a pleasant routine. He followed her to work every morning, and at work he found a thousand excuses to seek her out. They threw themselves into every project with more enthusiasm and energy than ever before. He wanted her opinion and approval on every decision he made. His hands-on approach to management left her the freedom to do what she loved—juggle numbers.

But much as she loved working with him, she looked more forward to their workday ending.

They would come back to her apartment together. When she closed the front door, and Keith would begin ripping off his tie and jacket, she would feel a leap of excitement. *For the first time, she felt as if someone belonged to her.*

They would cook dinner together, eat together, and she would usually do the dishes. They would talk, and before long—always when she had begun to monopolize their discussion or win their argument—he would start kissing her. Every day he gave her more pleasure than the day before. And it was only after he had fallen asleep in her arms that she would think of that awful first night when he had left her without a word. Then she would think of the future and the day he would walk out like that again—forever.

Besides that bleak future, what bothered her most about their life was that Keith stuck to his rule about Bobby Lee. Except for the times that Maggie brought Bobby Lee to the office, Kate didn't see much of the little boy. Some evenings after supper Keith would kiss Kate goodbye and go over to Maggie's to see his son. When Keith spent those first few Saturdays and Sundays away from her doing things with Bobby Lee, she missed them both unbearably.

She was feeling very depressed and lonely one Sunday when Keith came home early and found her. He saw her sad face and stunned her by asking her if they could have Bobby Lee over to eat supper and spend the night the next Friday night.

She was overjoyed and planned their supper down to the last detail. Then when Bobby Lee said what he really wanted was to go out for hamburgers, they went out instead. The evening went so wonderfully that Bobby Lee begged to stay the entire weekend with them. She begged, too, and Keith had reluctantly agreed.

After that weekend, Keith refused to let Bobby Lee spend another. Even so, Kate began to dream that Keith might really come to love her, that they might become a real family.

Keith teased her, he charmed her, he seduced her. But never once did he tell her he loved her. Sometimes when she was feeling down, she wondered if he made love to her so often because he wanted to get her pregnant so he could be rid of her. She began to wish she wouldn't get pregnant immediately, that their life would follow this idyllic pattern long enough for him to fall in love with her.

But one Monday morning she walked into the kitchen as Keith was frying bacon, and the thick sickening smell of bacon grease hit her like a heavy wave. For a second or two, as she groped to open the window and turn on the exhaust fan, she couldn't breathe.

As she gulped in fresh air, she thought she'd be okay. Then a second later, a stronger bout of nausea hit her. She swallowed and then dashed for the bathroom.

When the humiliating spasm had passed, Keith

helped her up. She felt even weaker and paler when she realized he had seen everything.

His handsome face was ashen. ''So—are we going to have a baby?''

''I—I think so.''

When she stared up at him forlornly, he pulled her into his arms and held her for a long moment as if she and the child were very precious to him. She clung, liking the way his hard hands were so gentle as they stroked her hair, wishing with all her heart that he would say he wanted to stay with her forever.

Instead, he let her go, his dark face tense again. ''Well, it looks like things are working out the way you wanted.''

''For you, too, I imagine.''

''This was your idea—not mine, remember?'' he said bitterly.

''Yes.''

And without another word, he turned and left her.

In spite of her joy over the baby, she felt doomed.

Chapter Ten

Keith had changed toward her drastically as soon as he'd learned about the baby. A new silent darkness had crept into their relationship.

Not that Keith was ever deliberately unkind. Not that Keith didn't support her in every imaginable way. Not that he hadn't helped her select a doctor and driven her to her checkups. Not that he wasn't endlessly patient with her mood swings and morning sickness. Not that he wasn't endlessly helpful when she was too tired to shop or do housework.

But there was a brooding quality about him now, a profound lethargy that seemed to drag him down. And her, too. He didn't laugh as much, and he was guarded and less spontaneous than before. Keith didn't insist she had to quit working as he had vowed he would, but as the months passed, she gradually turned more and more of her business affairs over to Keith and spent more of her time preparing for their baby.

With every day, Keith seemed to withdraw from her more. He came home later. He never initiated a conversation with her, and when she entered a room, he no longer looked up and smiled in the old way that had made her feel special.

Only at night, when they were in bed, did he now seem to belong to her. And even then, when he took her in his arms, she thought he did so reluctantly, as if he were fighting some part of himself, as if he were willing himself not to want her. But always when her mouth sought his, when her body surrendered to his, he melted, too, and their lovemaking bound some deep part of him to her, if only for those few fleeting moments of ecstasy. But afterward, he withdrew again and became that courteous stranger, who said the right things and did the right things. She would lie in the darkness, knowing that she was losing him and wondering what she could have done differently to have made him love her, wondering what was so wrong with her that no one had ever wanted her for herself alone.

Edwin had married her for her money, and so had Keith. The only difference was that Keith had been more brutally honest. He had never bothered to lie and say he loved her.

Even worse than her sleepless nights were the lonely weekends when Keith visited Bobby Lee. As the months sped by, her misery grew. Every Saturday morning when Keith left, she felt more abandoned than the one before. But she said nothing until one fateful Saturday a week or so before her due date.

That morning she felt heavy and irritable and dangerously moody and sorry for herself as she followed Keith to the living room. As he put his hand on the door to go, the pressure of the last few unhappy months mushroomed inside her. Suddenly she rushed up to him and, putting her hand on his, begged him to take her with him.

"Look," Keith began patiently enough. "I hate

leaving you all day—especially now, but you have my number...."

His number! Because her pregnancy played havoc with her hormones, she could swing from mildly dependent and needy to wildly hysterical at the speed of light. *She didn't want his number. She wanted him!*

You just don't get it, do you? She didn't speak aloud, but her sulky glare spoke volumes.

Her mind whirled even as she fought for control. How could he be so calm, so infuriatingly rational? It maddened her that his body wasn't bloated, that his emotions weren't in turmoil. Her whole life was changing and he was acting as if his wasn't and as if they still ought to be playing by the same old rules.

Not that it occurred to her that *she* had made the rules. In that self-pitying instant she hurtled over some precarious emotional edge. Suddenly she wanted to stomp up and down like a spoiled child and scream wildly. When her bottom lip curled sullenly, she bit down hard on it.

"Surely," he continued in that same, very male, hatefully rational tone, "you can see that your coming would just make this whole impossible situation more difficult—for all of us."

That did it!

Some tinsel-fine thread sheared at her emotional center.

"Impossible situation?" she shrieked. "I—Is that how you see our marriage? How you see me?" Then she began to weep, thinking even as the thick tears flowed down her puffy cheeks that the last thing she had wanted to do was scream and weep.

"And how do you see it, Kate?" he thundered, losing his patience at last. "I've often wondered. You made it damn clear that you didn't want a real marriage with me. Never—not once…except when we're in bed…have you ever acted— You're always so cool…so controlled." He started to say more and stopped himself. "I'd better go—before I do or say something we'll both regret!"

"Say it! Do it! What could be worse than the way you've been torturing me with your fake kindnesses, with—"

"Fake— Damn you, I'm not your robot, Kate— though I've tried to be. I'm a man, and I'm sick and tired of playing your game. You think you own the world…that you own me. You've told me about your father buying women. Are you really so different from him?"

"How…how can you say that?"

"Kate, I don't know if I can take another three or four months…." He turned to go.

"How can you just walk out?"

"With two feet, one after the other—darling."

"Oh, I—I do hate you."

His black eyes narrowed. "Is that really how you feel?"

She was too wild with her own pain to deny it. "Yes! Yes!"

His handsome face darkened. "Well, cheer up," he said quietly. "You will be rid of me soon enough. I regret this sham of a marriage every bit as much as you do." Without another word he stormed out, so anxious to leave he did not even bother to shut the front door.

She rushed after him and slammed it. Then in the next moment she pulled it open again. She wanted to call him back, to tell him that she didn't hate him, that she could never hate him, that she had only said that because he'd accused her of being like her father and because she was too proud to admit the truth— that she loved Keith and couldn't contemplate life without him.

But a savage pain tore through her middle and cut her in two. Gripping her distended abdomen in agony, she sank to the floor, calling after him helplessly.

But he had gone.

It was too late to tell him she loved him. She had lost him.

"Dear God, please don't let me lose his baby, too!"

She tried to get up, but a second fiery thrust slashed through her. She lay on the floor, panting breathlessly, fighting not to panic. But the pains were coming too hard and too fast, and she was terrified she would never make it to the hospital in time.

"Keith...I—I'm so sorry." Her voice was a whisper in the empty room. She shut her eyes and prayed silently.

From a long way away a deep voice said tenderly, "I'm sorry, too, my darling."

As if in a dream, hard, strong arms lifted her and cradled her close. She opened her eyes, and Keith was there. His dark face was quiet and grave.

He was her love. Her rock.

She reached for him and struggled to say something, but the pain cut off her breath.

"Don't try to talk," he whispered as he carried her out the door. "I'm taking you to the hospital."

The walls were white in the delivery room. Everyone wore blue. Even Keith, who was pressing her hand very tightly in his, was in blue.

A frightened voice cut through the haze of pain. "Doctor, I'm losing the baby's heartbeat!"

Kate clutched Keith's hand frantically and then started to scream. "No—not again!"

A mood of professional panic descended upon everyone.

"We're going to have to do a C-section."

A plastic mask was placed over Kate's face. She fought to shrug it off, but a gentle voice said firmly, "Sing the alphabet to me like a good girl."

When she got to the letter *C,* Keith's ashen, craggy face began to blur and float away. In a panic she realized she hadn't ever told him she loved him.

But when she tried to say the words, her voice died soundlessly. Then the lines of his dark face began to dissolve, and she was sliding away from the lights and the pain into a darkness that was total and eternal....

"You'll have to go now, Mr. Jones," a nurse ordered.

Keith nodded miserably even as he clutched Kate's lifeless hand more tightly. This was a thousand times worse than Mary because this was his fault. He had lost his temper and brought on the terrible fight that might end in Kate's death and his baby's. As he held on to her limp fingers, he vowed that if she lived, he would never allow himself to lose control again. He would stick to the idiotic bargain she had forced him to make—no matter what it cost him.

"If there's a choice, save *her*," Keith whispered desperately, knowing he was probably overreacting because of all the hospitals and all the surgeries he'd gone through with Mary. "Take the baby. But don't let her die. Please don't let her die."

"She's going to be fine, Mr. Jones."

Fighting to believe that, Keith leaned down and kissed Kate's cold pale cheek one last time. "Don't let her die—because I love her," he whispered.

But the woman who would have given anything for those words was asleep and did not hear them.

Chapter Eleven

"Where did you put my suitcase, Kate?" Keith called from the living room.

The long-expected question jolted through Kate as if it were a bolt out of the blue.

The sun was sparkling outside. Houston looked lovely. Kate had been leaning toward her mirror, running a brush nervously through her hair. At his simple query, every warm feeling inside her turned to ice. Her brush fell from her shaking fingers and clattered onto the bureau, scarring the fine glossy wood.

So today was to be the day he would walk out of her life forever.

Why today?

Heidi was four months old.

Kate had lived with the dread of this moment every day since Keith had brought her home from the hospital, her fear having intensified until that terrible third-month birthday.

But the dreaded date had come and gone, and although the day had been tense and she'd felt hysterically close to losing control, Keith had said nothing and done nothing. She had been too afraid to ask why because she might cause the very thing she feared most. And three days later Keith had even lovingly given her red roses on Mother's Day.

And now, suddenly, he was leaving her.

For a long moment she couldn't trust herself to answer in that cool polite manner that had become their custom—except for that one fight—ever since she'd gotten pregnant.

With the uncanny timing all babies are born with, Heidi started to cry.

Thank goodness! Relieved at the excuse not to answer him, Kate rushed to their daughter, only to find that Keith had gotten there first.

Kate paused at the door, unable to join him by the crib. "I just fed her and changed her." Her voice sounded lost and far away, not so carefully controlled—a stranger's voice.

Keith nodded absently and then grinned at the tiny redheaded being he gently lifted into his arms. "There, there, my sweet darling," he said to the baby in that husky, warm voice he never used with his wife—except in the dark when they made love.

Keith held the little girl close and continued to whisper soothingly. Only when Heidi began to coo did he speak to Kate again in that coolly polite tone. "I don't think she wants anything but love."

Dear God. Kate struggled to smile bravely in that cool way he was smiling at her, but her lips quivered.

Her heart was breaking. She was flying to pieces inside. The Karlington control, which had been her first line of defense against loneliness and despair, seemed to be shattering forever.

Not that he noticed. He had looked down at Heidi again, his entire cherishing attention focused on their daughter, who had wrapped her tiny fingers around his larger one.

Kate was not jealous of his love for Heidi. Kate simply wanted his love, too. And seeing how wonderful he was with their daughter always made Kate all the more sharply aware of his indifference to her.

Ever since Keith had brought them home from the hospital, he'd treated Kate as gingerly as she were made of eggshells. As if she were a stranger he was forced to live with and make polite conversation with. And she had played along, careful not to expose all her vulnerable new needs.

Not that he hadn't been wonderful. Those first weeks when she'd felt too weak and sick from the surgery, he had done practically everything for her and the baby. He allowed Bobby Lee to come more often now—to visit his sister. While Kate had been overly anxious about the baby because Heidi was her first, he, the more experienced parent, had been self-confident and relaxed. With every passing day, Kate had come to rely on his help and upon his steadiness and strength.

With every passing day she craved his love more.

"It's going to be hard not to see her every day," Keith murmured.

His low, polite voice sent a searing flash of pain through her. *It's going to be horrible not to see you every day, too,* she thought.

"I—I'll get your suitcase," Kate whispered and then stumbled upstairs to her hall closet, where she'd stashed it neatly all those long months ago. Frantically she began tearing boxes down from the packed shelves until she found it. Feeling wild and desperate, she tossed the hateful thing onto the landing, not caring when it rolled to the edge of the top stair, teetered and fell, end over end, banging loudly all the way down the winding stairs.

Miserably, Kate watched Keith come out of their daughter's room, lean down calmly and pick it up.

"Thanks. I guess I overstayed my welcome," he murmured mildly, not bothering to look up at her.

Thanks? After they'd lived together for more than a year?

Just go, if you're so anxious to! She wanted to shout at him. She wanted to run down the stairs and throw him and that awful suitcase out. But she was determined to avoid another wild humiliating scene like the one that had brought on her premature labor when he had said that he regretted their sham of a marriage.

Knowing she was on the verge of tears, Kate ran into her bathroom and locked the door so he wouldn't see. There she hugged herself against the wall and wept soundlessly as she listened to him throwing things into his bag. But as the tears rolled down her cheeks, in an odd way she was almost glad this thing she had dreaded had finally happened.

Because only now, when he was actually leaving, did she realize how unbearable the silent explosive tension between them had become. How had she borne needing him and wanting him this long while pretending that she was an aloof creature made of ice?

It seemed an eternity later that he uttered a muffled curse as he slammed his suitcase closed. Then she heard the sounds of his footsteps coming up the stairs.

She held her breath, struggling for control when he

hesitated before her door. After a long time he knocked gently.

"Kate—"

"Go away!" she whispered.

"I wanted to say…goodbye."

"Fine. Goodbye."

"You were the one who said that all you wanted from me was the baby."

"Yes," she whispered desperately, sinking to the floor like a broken lump, dying inside as she wondered how she would live without him.

"And that is still all you want, right? You want your perfect, neat life back, right?"

She choked on a sob. "Yes! Yes! Just go," she ground out in an agonized tone.

He hesitated and then she heard his retreating footsteps. They sounded like leaden weights going down.

The minute her front door slammed behind him, she unlocked the bathroom door and came flying out of it. Stepping onto the landing, she saw the heap of tangled boxes and hangers she'd thrown out of the closet. The silence in the vast apartment held a new and crushing loneliness. Gone were Keith's clothes thrown messily over the back of her couch.

Her gaze ran fondly to the plastic newspaper wrapper he'd left on the floor. More hot tears filled her eyes. It was the dearest thing in that room filled with priceless Karlington antiques.

Without Keith, the baby she had wanted so desperately would never be enough. The Karlington money meant nothing.

She hadn't ever wanted him to go. She had always

wanted him. As much as she had ever wanted their baby. *More.*

Then why hadn't she broken down and begged him to stay?

Because from the first she had been the one to chase him. Because she didn't want him to stay for any other reason except that he loved her. Because he had once said, "I regret this sham of a marriage...." Because she loved him enough to sacrifice her own happiness for his.

She was reasonably sure she could have used the baby and several other arguments to get him to stay. She had the Karlington money after all. She could have offered him the use of it, the power that came with it for as long as he stayed married to her.

She thought of the nights they shared in bed together. Of his final tendernesses to her when he'd taken her in his arms only the night before. Of his seeking mouth and roaming hands, his flaming passion. Of her own. But such passion was not love. Hadn't he told her she could have his body anytime— but never his soul?

She wanted all of him—desperately.

She wanted him to stay because he loved her.

Heidi began to cry.

Never again would she rush to her child and have the added pleasure of finding Keith there, too, to share her joy.

After a long moment Kate ran down the stairs. But when she opened the door to the nursery, Keith stepped coolly out of it.

Startled, caught completely off guard, she felt terribly vulnerable—exposed. Her voice came out harshly, defensively. "What are you still doing here?"

But he was different, too. The cool stranger was gone. She saw an agony as wild and profound as her own in his piercing black eyes as he stared at her tear-streaked face.

"Why are you crying?" he demanded in a gentle, compassionate tone.

"I—I'm not…cry…ing," but the words came out in a horrendous very un-Karlington-like blubber. "I don't want you to pity me…."

In the next minute, his arms came around her, and his searching mouth claimed hers hotly, passionately—adoringly.

"God, Kate, I tried to leave you—"

Heidi made a muffled, indignant sound.

"What about the baby—" she whispered brokenly as he propelled her into the hall and slammed the door.

"The baby is fine. We've both spoiled her—that's all."

"I don't understand. Why…why are you still here?"

"Because, damn you, I'm not a high-class Karlington who can say goodbye to you through a locked door. Because I can't play by your rules another miserable second," he said brokenly, angrily. "Because I want you too much to let you go without a fight. I don't care if you despise me because I'm poor…and you're rich. If you despise me because you think you bought me or because you think I'm a failure or because I made this stupid idiotic deal. Or because your family thinks I'm a gold digger—''

''But I—I don't think any of those awful things. I—I don't despise you. I—I made all those stupid rules to protect myself...because I'd been hurt before. I—I thought you regretted our marriage.''

He didn't seem to hear her. ''I want to help you raise Heidi. I feel like a heel leaving you to face it all—practically alone—even if it is your idea. I don't go for the mother of my kid raising my kid alone when she doesn't have to.''

''You don't have to go,'' she said, no longer caring that she was chasing him again. ''I never wanted you to.''

''I thought you just wanted me to serve as a baby machine.''

''No. I love you, Keith. I've always loved you. That's probably why I wanted your baby that first night, why I asked you to marry me. Why I did all the stupid things I've done.''

''I'm glad you did those things. Because I love you, too,'' he said simply. ''I have for a long time.''

''Are you sure you want me...and not my money?''

''Damn your money and your father and Edwin for making you think money is everything. I wish you were poor. That we were equal.''

''We are equal,'' she whispered. ''More than equal. I think you're wonderful.''

He kissed her mouth softly, reverently. ''I love you for yourself alone. You are everything to me.''

A long time later, after many fervent kisses, she

asked, "If you loved me so much, why didn't you ever tell me before?"

"Because I was playing by your rules. Suffering under them. Dying under them. When I gave you that ring, you reminded me we wouldn't have a real marriage. After that... Then the one time I broke down, we had that terrible fight and you went into labor. I was so afraid you might die...that the baby might die...that it would be all my fault...that I decided to stick to your stupid rules till you told me to go. I did it for you. I didn't want to ever hurt you like that again."

"Oh, my darling. I thought...you were just marking off the days till you could leave me."

"After you got pregnant, I hated every day and every night we had together, because time was our enemy. Then, when Heidi was three months old and you didn't throw me out, I began to hope you felt something for me, too. But you never said— Not even when I gave you the roses on Mother's Day. You were just this exquisite polite stranger who said, 'Thank you, darling.'"

"You didn't say anything, either. Why did you pick today to leave?"

"Today?" He raked his hands through his hair. "I just couldn't take it anymore. I couldn't live with you—loving you, wanting you to love me. And I could see what this was doing to Bobby Lee. Every time he came to stay, he begged to stay. He feels left out."

"I do love both of you. I wanted him with us so much. But I was afraid to show it...especially after you left me on our wedding night. I thought maybe I'd chased too hard and been too eager...."

"I left because I realized I was madly in love with you, and I didn't know how I could live with you and not let on. I left because I loved you, but I came back for the same reason. It's why I couldn't walk out the door today."

"And I was too proud to confess how much I loved you partly because I'd chased you so blatantly, so shamelessly."

"Honey, I want you to chase me—for the rest of our lives. I like it when you're shameless."

And the incredible warmth in his voice lit a tiny spark of happiness within her that soon grew into a fire that raged out of control when he carried her up to bed. For the first time in a long time they made love in the middle of the day with the sunlight streaming through the high windows. And she lost all control, gave herself to him more shamelessly than ever before.

Afterward she wouldn't let him go until he admitted that at last she did possess every part of him— not only his body but his soul, as well.

And he possessed every part of her, too.

Keith loved her. She was the mother of his children.

But most of all, she was his beloved wife.

* * * * *

Escape into

Just a few pages
into any Silhouette®
novel and you'll find
yourself escaping
into a world of
desire and intrigue,
sensation and
passion.

Silhouette

SILHOUETTE®

Escape into

Enjoy the drama, explore the emotions, experience the relationship.

Longer than other Silhouette® books, Superromance™ offers you emotionally involving, exciting stories, with a touch of the unexpected

Four new titles are available every month on subscription from the

READER SERVICE™

GEN/38/RS

Escape into

Vivid, satisfying romances, full of family, life and love.

Special Edition™ are romances between attractive
men and women. Family is central to the plot. The
novels are warm upbeat dramas grounded in reality
with a guaranteed happy ending.

Six new titles are available every month on
subscription from the

READER SERVICE™

Escape into

Intense, sensual love stories.

Desire™ are short, fast and sexy romances featuring alpha males and beautiful women. They can be intense and they can be fun, but they always feature a happy ending.

Six new titles are available every month on subscription from the

READER SERVICE™

Escape into

Passionate, dramatic, thrilling romances.

Sensation™ are sexy, exciting, dramatic and thrilling romances, featuring dangerous men and women strong enough to handle them.

Six new titles are available every month on subscription from the

READER SERVICE™